LAURA SPIVAK

When Evelyn Sleeps

Bear Pond
PRESS

First published by Bear Pond Press 2023
Copyright © 2023 by Laura Spivak

First edition
ISBN: 979-8-9894758-0-3
Cover art by Getcovers Design
Editing by Enchanted Inkwell
Author photograph by Michelle Peirce Photography

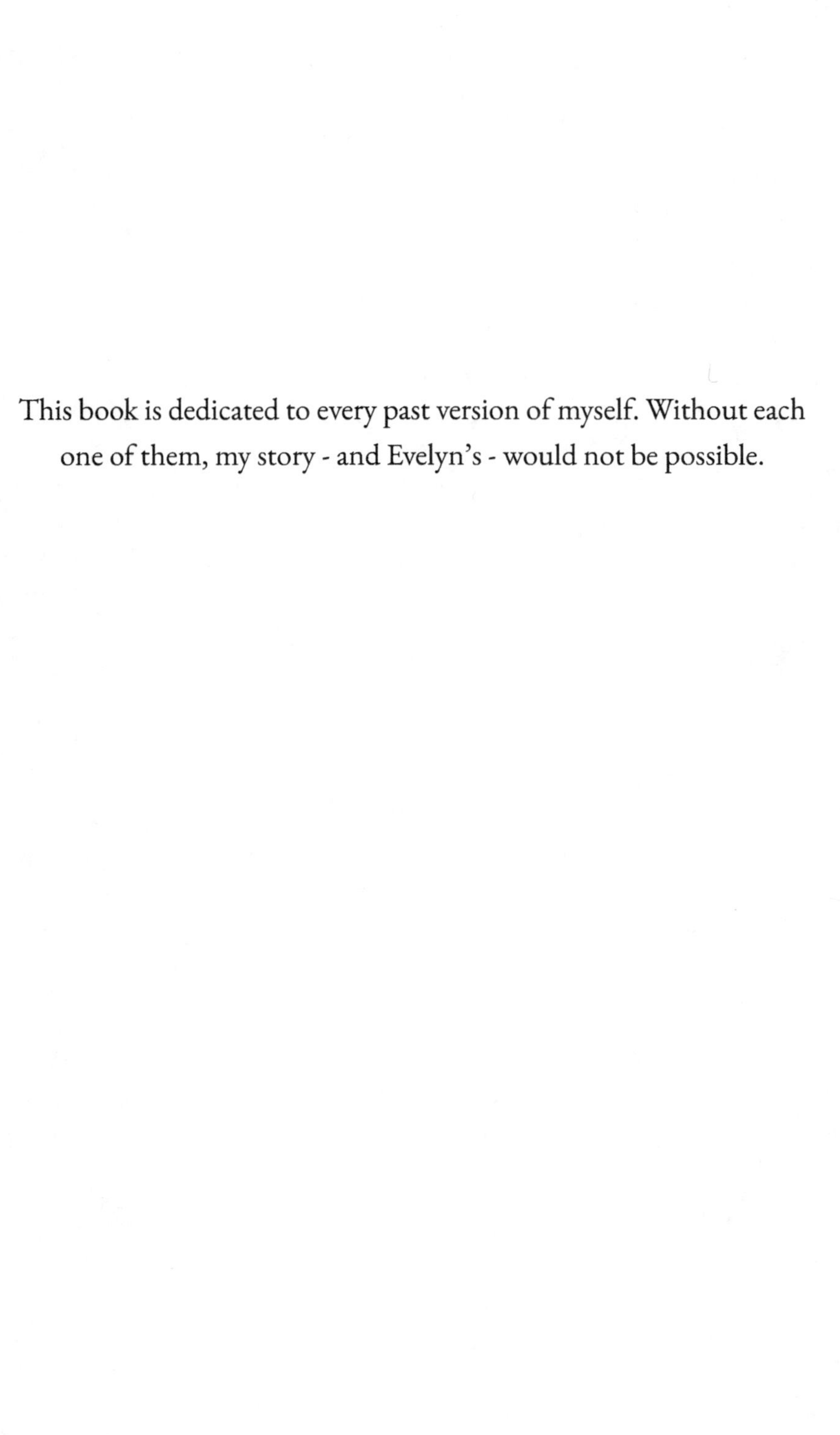

This book is dedicated to every past version of myself. Without each one of them, my story - and Evelyn's - would not be possible.

Chapter 1
1919

In her other life, Evelyn Moore would have eviscerated the man who'd just laughed in her face when she'd mentioned women's voting rights. Instead, she made a sarcastic excuse and abandoned the outdoor party to hide on a velvet bench in the foyer. The rush of adrenaline still coursing through her from not being able to verbally dress him down had left her shaking with rage. She was proud of her work in the women's voting movement, and their victory earlier that year was a highlight of Evelyn's life. It infuriated her that some people still saw it as a joke.

After a few minutes of welcome solitude spent taking in the beauty of the ornate mansion, she stood and smoothed her dress, preparing to rejoin the party.

Evelyn headed through the glittering crowd to where she had last seen her friends. As she moved further away from the jazz band, she heard her friend Emily's distinct, shrill voice call her name.

"Ev! Over here!" Emily, Lily, and Ada were standing around a tall table covered in a sparkling champagne-colored tablecloth.

"Isn't this house gorgeous?" Emily gushed, gripping Evelyn's upper arm and pulling her closer.

"Like out of one of my magazines!" Evelyn admired the setting. "But you know we have to get out of here soon, don't you?" The girls all groaned dramatically in unison, knowing Evelyn was right. Some of them had work in the morning. Evelyn had warned them earlier in the night—before the drinks started flowing—that they had to leave the party no later than one o'clock.

"How about one more drink and a quick tour of the eligible bachelors before we go?" asked Lily, playfully poking Evelyn's shoulder, taunting her with the possibility of a few last minutes of fun.

Evelyn knew she should refuse, but when she saw her friends' expectant faces, she sarcastically rolled her eyes, sighing in agreement. "Fine!" She smiled. "But just once around the yard. Then we're out of here!" They were so excited to be at their first party in almost two years. The past eighteen months had been very touch-and-go for the entire country, and now that the restrictions from the flu pandemic were lifting, the young people wanted to embrace all the freedom they could at this party.

The group of friends cheered and made their way to the patio, where Ada was quick to spot a young man who had been chatting her up earlier. She convinced him to get a round of Sidecars for the four women, saving them a trip to the bar. Once their beverages were in hand, Ada skillfully waved off her admirer and told him she would see him later, knowing she wouldn't. The women walked two-by-two, making a slow circle around the beautifully landscaped yard, a rare gem in a city like New York where having a yard typically meant you enjoyed a postage stamp-sized patch of grass next to your front door. An impressive marble fountain served as the centerpiece of the bustling party.

Evelyn scanned the crowd half-interested as they walked through the space, stopping occasionally to make small talk with acquaintances. She wanted nothing more than to go home and get into bed. She hurried her friends to the back porch and through the massive sliding glass doors. Urging the girls to gather their coats, Evelyn hustled them toward the front door but took a moment to soak in some of the beauty of the home. She craned her neck, taking in an elaborate crystal chandelier hanging above the doorway.

"You'll get your fancy house one day! Come on, Ev!" Ada joked as the group exited the elegant townhome onto the sidewalk of Fifty-Sixth Street.

"I'll start saving for it tomorrow!" Evelyn laughed. She glanced back at the front door of the house, making a mental note of the chandelier and its features. Crystals hung from its rectangular frame, glittering as the wind from the street whipped in through the front door. "Let's go!"

An hour later, ready for bed, Evelyn stood at her living room window admiring the city view for a few moments before drawing the curtains closed. As she made her way back to her bedroom, a framed photo of her great aunt Mavis on the end table caught her eye. Evelyn had come to New York a year ago after her great aunt had passed away and surprisingly left her beautiful one-bedroom apartment to Evelyn's parents. Great Aunt Mavis had known how badly Evelyn longed to live in the city and requested that her parents allow her to move into the apartment and begin working her way into a good career. Evelyn had jumped at the chance.

She climbed into bed and set her alarm for seven o'clock, doing the math in her head. She would only have a few hours to sleep. She leaned over to her nightstand and picked up her dream journal, scribbling on the corner of the page to get her pen working.

The party tonight was fabulous. The mansion, the gardens, the lights, the fountain, the music. All perfect. So why was I distracted? Part of me wonders if I'll ever have a house even half as nice as that, or anyone to share it with, since men here seem so preoccupied with their own egos. Tonight I met a rather handsome young man who was very sweet to me until he found out I was a women's voting activist. He immediately stopped taking me seriously. I was so angry I had to take a moment to myself in the foyer. I began thinking about my romantic future. I hope someday I'll find someone in this city who isn't terrified of a woman who has convictions and ambitions beyond simply getting married. I want to do something important.

In my other life—in my dreams—it's a lot easier for women to follow their desires. So much progress has already been made. We can go to universities, hold positions of power, and are free to pursue relationships without the restrictive social boundaries of 1919. Some days I long for that freedom here, and it can be difficult going back and forth between having equality and being scorned for seeking it. Still, I find myself lonely and hopeful that I will eventually find a man here in 1919 who can handle my independent streak.

    P.S. I saw a chandelier at the mansion I am putting on my shopping list for my future house!

Evelyn sketched a crude drawing of the light fixture so she'd remember it before replacing her journal on her nightstand.

If nothing else, she thought, her double life was a great story, and maybe she would write a book someday from the contents of her journals. She didn't know why, exactly, but keeping a record of her dreams was important to Evelyn. She hoped it would serve her one day, even though she wasn't sure how.

Silently wondering if anyone else was as deeply in tune with their dreams as she was, she snuggled into bed. Forcing her eyes shut, Evelyn rushed as quickly as she could into her other world, where she spent half her life.

Chapter 2
2003

The alarm on her flip phone went off at eight a.m. sharp. Evelyn reached over and turned off the annoying tone. Phone still in hand, she buried her cheek further into her satin pillowcase as she fought not to fall asleep again. Willing her brain not to descend back into her dreams, she began to go over her plans for the day.

"Morning classes, Campus Anti-war Network meeting at lunch, afternoon class," Evelyn whispered aloud to herself. "Date night!" Her eyes popped open as she remembered tonight's plans with her boyfriend, Cole, and she was out of bed and starting her morning routine in under a minute. She was excited but slightly nervous as she thought about what he might have planned for their one-year anniversary. She'd dropped so many hints about things she'd like to do to celebrate a year together, but he'd never been great at taking her hints. Traditional romance wasn't Cole's strong suit, but she still hoped he'd come through for this special occasion.

A few hours later, Evelyn arrived at the dining hall for her meeting with the anti-war group she had founded on campus. She had formed it as part of a nationwide grassroots movement to promote anti-war activism for people her age after the United States had dropped its first bomb on Baghdad earlier in the year. She and a classmate from some of her political science courses had managed to corral a few like-minded individuals to come up with ideas and events that could increase awareness on campus and throughout the city. They were working on a protest outside the United Nations building that would take place in a few days.

She scanned the busy dining area and headed toward the far wall, where she had a table reserved for her group's meeting that day. A few of the members had already seated themselves and were chatting as she made her way over. Evelyn's cofounder, Will, stood to greet her with a friendly hug. He had transferred from another school during their junior year, and they'd met in an international relations class. He was slightly taller than she was, and physically not her typical type, but Evelyn always got a little flip in her stomach when they talked, though she would never admit it out loud. She and Will were just friends. His thoughtful eyes and passion for the cause were attractive qualities, but Evelyn was committed to Cole and was not entertaining other relationships.

"How did you do on that paper in O'Connell's class?" Will asked, sitting back down in his chair. Evelyn winced at the question.

"Honestly? Probably could have done better." She didn't want to tell him she had gotten an embarrassing C+ on the paper. She had been a little distracted with Cole when she should have been paying attention to her schoolwork, if she was being honest.

She called the meeting to order. "Okay, everyone. Thanks for coming. Will, do you have the information printed out for the rally?"

"Sure do." He grabbed a stack of papers from the table in front of him. He handed them out to the group members as Evelyn continued speaking.

"So, we have the anti-war rally at the UN building coming up on Monday, which is only a couple of days away." She opened her notebook and jotted down the date. "Before then, each of us will have a job to do to make sure this protest goes off safely and without a hitch." Evelyn went down the list and assigned each member a specific duty to complete before Monday's planned student protest. As the mastermind behind the event, she was nervous and excited that the big day was approaching.

When the meeting wrapped up, Evelyn and Will stuck around for a few minutes to discuss the details of the protest and make sure everything was ready. She was impressed that he had printed out a to-do list for the event. She was confident that together, they could actually pull it off. When there was nothing left to say about the rally, the two sat in a brief, awkward silence. Will broke the tension, asking Evelyn where she was headed next.

"Just art history, then I have to go home and get ready for an anniversary date with my boyfriend," she replied.

"Sounds fun. Congrats! What are you two doing to celebrate?"

"Actually, I'm not sure." She laughed. "He's in charge of planning the date, so I have no idea what to expect!"

"Oh, risky move on your part! Just kidding. I'm sure it'll be great."

"Here's hoping!" Evelyn checked the clock on her phone. "I gotta run. I'm going to be late for class!"

She gathered her things, said goodbye to Will, and went about her day, counting down the hours until her date. Cole was like the guys she had always gone for. Dark, rebellious, and a little dangerous, but with what she thought was a good heart, which Cole seemed to reserve exclusively for when they were alone. Her relationships had historically all become exhausting because she'd spent so much time defending them to her friends and family, and this one was no different.

Her best friend, Cammie, was Cole's biggest critic. Cammie loved Evelyn. They'd known each other since ninth grade and ended up at college together. They were protective of each other, and Cammie thought Cole was controlling and inattentive. Still, Evelyn believed that with time, Cammie and everyone else would see the softer side of Cole and understand their relationship better.

Even though Cammie couldn't stand Cole, she was always willing to give fashion advice, so on the bus ride back to her apartment, Evelyn called her.

"What's up Ev?"

"What do I wear tonight when I have no idea where I'm going?" Evelyn asked, trying not to speak too loudly.

"Knowing Cole? Nothing too fancy," Cammie quipped.

"I don't know. I've been hinting at some places I want to go, so I'm hoping he was listening!"

"Ev, he *never* listens to you. That's one reason I can't officially endorse this relationship as your BFF. You know that."

Evelyn sighed. "I know."

As though sensing her best friend's exasperation, Cammie switched her tone. "I think you should wear a little black dress and a jean jacket. You can't go wrong with a little black dress no matter what restaurant he takes you to!"

"LBD it is! Thank you. I'll call you after the date and let you know how it went."

"You'd better!" Cammie hung up before Evelyn could reply.

She smiled, knowing Cammie would support her in spite of her dislike for Cole but wishing she could get her friend and her boyfriend on the same page.

That evening, with the sun setting in the bedroom window behind her, Evelyn stood at the mirror, painstakingly applying makeup and curling her hair, waiting for Cole. A few minutes later, as she finished zipping up her dress, Cole called to tell her he was outside. She grabbed her purse and draped a denim jacket over her shoulders, rushing out of her apartment to take the elevator to the first floor.

He had gotten out of the car to open the passenger door for her by the time she arrived at the curb, which was surprising considering chivalry was not Cole's forte. She gave him a light kiss as she greeted him. "Happy anniversary." She smiled sweetly, lowering herself into the car, ready for what she was beginning to think might turn out to be a memorable night.

Chapter 3

2003

"So, where are you taking me?" Evelyn asked, playfully raising her eyebrows as Cole buckled his seat belt.

He started the car. "Wouldn't you like to know?"

She agreed not to ask any more questions and wait for the surprise. She turned on the radio, searching for a song they both liked. Their tastes in music rarely met in the middle. He liked heavy metal, and she was more a classic rock girl. She gave up after a few tries and clicked it off, sitting back in her seat.

After about twenty minutes of rather silent driving through the city, Cole finally parallel parked his car in a tiny spot along Sixth Avenue. Evelyn waited for him to open her door like he had when he'd picked her up, and a few moments passed before she realized he was waiting on the sidewalk for her to do it herself. She climbed out of the car, trying to figure out where they were going. About half a block away, a line of people waited to get into a restaurant whose name she couldn't read from her vantage point.

"Don't worry, we don't have to wait in line. I know a guy." Cole winked and began walking. Evelyn hurried after him, struggling to keep up in her heels. They passed the crowd waiting to enter and approached the hostess at the door. Evelyn still didn't know where she was, but she was impressed that Cole had thought ahead to make a reservation.

"Hey, I'm Cole Harrison. My friend Matt works here, and he told me he'd have a table for me tonight for my anniversary."

"Harrison . . . let me see." The hostess looked over her list. "I don't see it here. I'm sorry, who did you say reserved your table?"

"Matt."

She smirked. "Matt, the new busboy?"

"I guess," Cole answered.

"Matt can't just promise tables to people, and I don't have your reservation on my list." She pursed her lips, clearly unsure of what to do in this awkward situation.

"Okay, well, that's not true, because he told me all I had to do was mention his name and we'd have a table."

"Unfortunately, sir, we're full right now and, as you can see, we have a line of people waiting to get in. I can't just push you ahead of them because you're friends with the busboy."

Cole's face turned red with anger, and Evelyn was embarrassed that this was all happening with her on his arm. She worried he would make a scene. This was just the type of scenario that usually riled him up, and she didn't want the night to end with another one of Cole's outbursts.

"It's fine, we'll wait in the line. Thank you!" Evelyn spoke up, pulling Cole from the restaurant door and toward the back of the line.

"What are you doing? I was handling it!" Cole yanked his arm from her grasp.

"It's not worth it. The line is moving pretty quickly. Let's just people-watch and talk while we wait!"

Cole rolled his eyes and joined her at the end of the queue. She tried making small talk to lighten his mood, but his ego had been bruised and it was going to take more than idle chatter to raise his spirits. It dawned on her that she still didn't know what they were in line for. Some of the people ahead of them were families with small children.

"So, what is this restaurant, anyway?"

Cole's mood lifted as he realized his big reveal had arrived.

"Jekyll and Hyde!" he announced proudly.

"What?" Evelyn raised her eyebrows.

"The Jekyll and Hyde Club!" He obviously assumed she had heard of it. Noting the blank stare on her face, he explained. "It's like a haunted mansion inside, with actors in costumes and talking paintings on the wall. You get to watch a whole show while you eat! It's awesome!"

She was shocked he would think she'd enjoy such a place. She hated horror movies and ghost stories, and she had made her opinion on theme restaurants clear when he'd dragged her to a Mars theme restaurant in Times Square where the costumed aliens had been a little too aggressive for Evelyn's taste. They'd relentlessly interrupted their meal and gunned for tips every time they came to the table. She cringed at the memory and hoped this would be better.

Her hopes were dashed as soon as they sat down at their table where a talking rhinoceros head mounted on the wall complimented Evelyn on her outfit and joked about stealing Cole's date from him. She was irked by the idea that whoever was behind that creepy rhino could be sitting there the entire time they were eating and could hear their conversation. Cole, on the other hand, thought the rhino was hilarious and appeared unbothered by its presence on their date. Evelyn could understand why children and families would enjoy the restaurant, but she was flummoxed by Cole's decision to celebrate their anniversary in such a loud, over-the-top venue.

Soon, Cole caught sight of Matt, the infamous busboy. He greeted Cole with a high five and failed to greet Evelyn at all.

"Hey, sorry about the mix-up with the table. The hostess must have forgotten to put it on the list."

"It's no problem, man. I appreciate you hooking us up!"

Evelyn said nothing. She wasn't buying Matt's excuses, but Cole was eating them up.

"What time do you get off work?" he asked Matt, causing Evelyn to raise her eyebrows.

Matt checked his watch. "About thirty minutes."

"Come join us when you're done!"

Evelyn's heart dropped. Cole had a history of letting his friends interrupt their dates. They'd fought about it several times. Of all the dates to invite his buddies to join, this was the last one she'd have expected. She didn't want to offend Matt, so she kept quiet until he was gone. "Are you sure it's a good idea to invite Matt to join us on our anniversary date?" She tried not to sound too angry.

"We'll be done eating. What's the problem?" He was genuinely clueless.

"I'm sorry, I thought we might be able to get through dessert before one of your buddies crashed another one of our dates," she snapped a little more harshly than she'd intended. She didn't mind his friends, but the sheer rudeness of never asking her if they could join their dates irritated her. She sighed to herself and decided to let it go. Maybe when they exchanged gifts after dinner the night would take a better turn. She'd gotten him something she hoped he'd really like, and she was excited for his reaction.

After spending a long few drinks with Matt in the noisy, decidedly unromantic restaurant, Cole and Evelyn returned home. She was lucky to live alone in New York at her age. She'd received such a good scholarship her parents had allowed her to use her college savings for rent on a small apartment close to campus. She sometimes wondered if she was missing out on dorm life and roommates, but if she surrounded herself with distractions, she would lose the scholarship she'd worked so hard for.

Cole opened a bottle of red wine he found on the kitchen counter and poured them each a glass. She'd only had one drink at the restaurant and didn't feel much like drinking now, but she took the glass from him anyway. He probably wouldn't notice whether she drank it or not. He and Matt had indulged in several stiff beverages before they left Jekyll and Hyde, and Evelyn had been forced to drive Cole's car back afterward. She had hoped Cole might think to bring her some champagne, knowing it was her favorite, but she realized this night may have been more momentous for her than it had ever been for him.

"Cheers," they both said, clinking their wine glasses together. Cole took a sip and, as Evelyn expected, did not notice that Evelyn didn't sip hers. He scrunched his face and sputtered. "Ugh! I don't know how you drink this stuff!" They settled on the living room couch, and wanting to stop him from instinctively reaching for the TV remote, Evelyn quickly suggested they exchange gifts, hoping it would be the pick-me-up her night—and her relationship—needed. Cole stood up to retrieve something from his coat. He clutched a plain white envelope as he made his way back to the couch and sat down.

Evelyn reached into her handbag on the floor next to her, pulling out a small box wrapped in red paper with silver hearts along with a card in a hand-decorated envelope. "You wanna go first?"

He ripped the paper off without opening the card. Biting her tongue, she waited anxiously. She had gone to a lot of trouble to get this gift for him, and she was hoping he would be as thrilled to receive it as she was to give it to him. He finally opened it, furrowing his brow in confusion. "A guitar pick?"

"Well yeah, but it's not just a regular one," Evelyn replied, perhaps a little louder than she'd meant to. She lowered her voice. "It's one that was used by the lead singer of that band you love, Nuclear Assault! I won it on an eBay auction. I've never even done an eBay auction before!" She paused, waiting for a reaction from him. "I hope you like it?"

"Yeah. It's really cool. Thanks, babe." He turned it over in his hand. "I would never have thought to ask for a used guitar pick as a gift."

She tried to maintain a good poker face. "It's not just a used guitar pick," she said, making air quotes as she talked. "It's actual memorabilia from your favorite guitarist. It's a collectible. I thought you would like it."

"No, no. It's really awesome. I love it, I promise." He held his gift out. "Here, open yours."

Evelyn took the white letter-sized envelope, noting it was certainly not a greeting card, and slid her finger under the flap to tear it open. Pulling out two tickets, she smiled, thinking they must be for the MET fashion exhibit she'd been wanting to see. She'd dropped so many hints she couldn't imagine he hadn't figured it out. Turning them over, her heart sank.

"The New York International Auto Show?" Her shoulders dropped in dismay.

"Yeah! You said you wanted to learn more about cars so you would know what I was talking about all the time. I figured this would be a great way for you to learn!" The excitement on Cole's face was almost too much for her to bear. After a year he really didn't know her at all.

"Wow! Great idea," she lied. Of all the things Evelyn cared about, cars were low on the list. She was having a hard time feigning a good mood at this point in the night. It wasn't just the wrong date or the wrong gift. It was becoming evident to Evelyn that Cole might be the wrong guy. Wanting the evening to end as soon as possible so she could just go to sleep, she got up and went to the kitchen, making a show of searching the cabinets for something. When Cole asked, she told him she was looking for Aspirin.

"I'm not feeling that great, actually. I might need to go to bed and sleep off this headache I'm getting." Thankfully, he took the hint for once.

"I'll let you go to bed." He grabbed his jacket from the back of the couch. "Some of the guys are down at the bar."

Evelyn walked Cole to the apartment door. "Thank you for dinner and the gift. Happy anniversary," she said, mustering all the sincerity she could. They kissed and said goodnight, and she closed the door, locking it behind him. She was in disbelief over the difference between the night she had pictured and the night she'd actually had. She had some thinking to do about her relationship with Cole, but right now, all she wanted to do was go to bed.

She opened her journal, wishing she didn't have to document the night, but she picked up her pen and began writing anyway.

Well, it turns out a year with a person isn't enough time to get to know them at all. My anniversary date with Cole was a disaster. It was like he thought of all the things I would hate and planned them all for one night. He took me to a cheesy theme restaurant where he spent half the time talking about sports with his friend. The gift he picked is obviously more for him than it is for me, and I'm starting to think the relationship itself is just as unbalanced.

I don't want Cammie and everyone else to be right about Cole, but I think I'm beginning to agree that he may not be the right match for me. Still, I do love him, and I know he has a good side. I just wish I—and the rest of the world—could see it more often. Dreading calling Cammie tomorrow to tell her about the date.

Evelyn closed her journal and quickly drifted to sleep, happy to leave Cole and hoping she'd have a better day in her dreams.

Chapter 4
1919

Evelyn was downcast when she woke up for work. She couldn't stop thinking about how disappointed she was that the man in her dreams let her down so much. How could Cole have bungled their anniversary so badly? Retrieving a letter from her mother on her way out helped lift her spirits a bit. She read it while she waited to cross the street at a busy intersection.

Dearest Evelyn,

It's been a while since we've had a letter from you. I hope things in New York are still going well. We miss you, but we know how important it is for you to be in the city.

Your father says to tell you hello. He also wants you to know he is hard at work growing what he is certain will be the prize-winning squash at this year's fair!

Evelyn folded the letter and went across the road. She would have to finish reading it later. She smiled to herself as she recalled helping her father grow prize-worthy produce in their garden every year and all the blue ribbons they'd collected together at the county fair. Evelyn did love her life back home, but there was a part of her that could never be fulfilled living in rural Virginia. She made a mental note to write to her parents soon. Her mother was right. It had been a while.

As she walked briskly to the office, Evelyn was so lost in her thoughts she barely noticed the rain that had begun lightly falling. She popped her umbrella up over her head and quickened her pace.

She swung open the heavy door to the office building where she worked and forced her brain to switch gears from her dreams to her reality: her job as a secretary for a busy attorney who paid her well but expected her work ethic to match. Mr. Allen had been a lawyer in the city for over twenty years, and while he was a compassionate man, he also ran a tight ship. They'd met when he offered his legal services pro bono to the women's voting movement as they fought for the cause. They'd clicked instantly, and when his previous secretary died of the Spanish Flu, he hired Evelyn, impressed by her drive and dedication to voting rights.

Though she had only been working for him a little over a year, Evelyn had become strangely close with her boss. Mr. Allen had grown fond of her as well and had turned into something of a father figure for her. He genuinely cared about her wellbeing and success. In many ways he reminded her of her own father.

In spite of their disdain for metropolitan life, Evelyn's parents had graciously allowed her to move into the apartment Great Aunt Mavis had left them in New York so Evelyn could attend secretarial school. Now that she was working for Mr. Allen, she was paying her own way in the city, something she was very proud of. It wasn't common for an unwed woman in 1919 to have her own place in New York, and while it gave her a powerful confidence most women in the city did not enjoy, she wondered if it made her intimidating or undesirable to a lot of the men she'd met since she moved there. They always seemed to shy away when they learned she was so independent, and she had yet to meet someone who was secure enough in his own life to be comfortable with her forward-thinking ideals. Perhaps even one who didn't scoff at the idea of women having an equal vote or women having opinions about the Great War.

Evelyn wished the United States had stayed out of the Great War completely but also found it shocking that after everything the country had been through during the conflict, there was even still a question that women should have an equal vote. So many women had sacrificed their time, energy and home lives to fill the manufacturing jobs left vacant by men sent to fight on the front lines. Sadly, even the war had not been enough to convince the strongest women's suffrage opponents, and the fight had raged on until women were finally granted equal voting rights earlier in the year. The last few years had been a whirlwind of current events that had left the country—and most of the people in it—changed somehow. Evelyn was sure it had changed her for the better. She'd become firmer in her resolve to make a difference and to rise above what this world had decided women could and should do. She'd gotten a taste of what real freedom felt like in her other timeline, and she was increasingly unwilling to settle for less in this one.

From her desk, Evelyn heard Mr. Allen rustling and rummaging around in his office. He soon emerged, clad in his raincoat and hat. His face lit up when he saw her. "Good morning! Hope you didn't stay out too late last night!" He jokingly wagged his finger at her.

"Me? Never!" she replied, feigning offense.

"I'm headed out to get a bagel and the paper. Can I get you anything?"

Most attorneys in the Big Apple sent their secretaries out to get their bagels and newspapers for them, but Mr. Allen insisted on running his own personal errands, claiming he needed the exercise. She politely declined, and he went on his way. Evelyn took the opportunity alone in the office to jot down everything she could remember about her dream of her awful date with Cole the night before.

The dream was still bothering her, as they sometimes did. When this happened, she usually turned to writing to get her thoughts out. The pages of her dream journals told the story of a girl who lived during the millennium, eighty-four years in the future. She often wondered how much of what her subconscious dreamed up about the world would end up coming true in eighty years or so. There was obviously no way to know, but if she asked other people about it, they might think she was insane. Her parents had never believed that she could see the future in her dreams when she was a little girl. She wished they had listened to her talk about her dreams more, since they were so real and important to her. She'd followed her parents' advice anyway and kept her dreams to herself, not wanting anyone to think she was out of her mind. In both timelines her parents had dismissed her as thinking up wild stories and sent her off to play. The same reaction every time she tried, until she eventually learned at a young age not to bring it up anymore in either of her lives. That was when she had started keeping dream journals. She figured maybe someday someone would believe her, and perhaps if she documented everything she could prove she wasn't making it all up. She closed the journal with a thud and shook her head quickly to get focused before she tackled a pile of work Mr. Allen had left on her desk earlier.

Evelyn was packing up to go home from work when raindrops began tapping on the office window.

"Perfect," she muttered to herself, wrapping her journal in her handkerchief to keep it from the rain before putting it back into her bag. She popped her head around the corner into Mr. Allen's office, knocking lightly on the open door. "Do you need anything before I go?"

"Are you sure you want to leave right now?" He turned to face his office window and gestured toward the rain. "It's bucketing out there!"

"I'll be fine! I have my umbrella and my flat shoes, see?" She showed him her low-heeled black leather shoes with the pointed toe.

He chuckled, making a quizzical face. "You call those flats?"

"Don't worry, I have lots of practice!" Evelyn laughed. "Have a good weekend. See you on Monday!" She hurried out of the office and took the stairs down to the sidewalk. The building's heavy door creaked as she pushed it open, exposing herself to the rain, which was much heavier than it had looked from upstairs. She opened her umbrella and weighed which way to go. A shortcut through the alley across from her building would shorten her walk by almost a block.

She clutched her coat tightly at her chest with one hand, holding her umbrella with the other, her bag slung over her arm. She hurried down the short stretch of pavement and ducked into the alley. Goosebumps immediately covered her body. This alley, like most, was probably not the best place for a young lady on her own, but she had taken it many times before in the rain and had never run into a soul.

Evelyn had been so paranoid when she had initially moved to the city, always glancing over her shoulder and triple-checking every lock on her doors and windows before bed. She'd heard so many horror stories about big cities from her parents that she was surprised at how quickly she had felt at home in the bustling place. She knew it wasn't ever going to be totally secure. Nowhere was—especially for single women—but Evelyn had become used to these metropolitan surroundings and no longer found herself compelled to spend every second worrying about her safety.

Trying to avoid dirty rainwater, she kept her head down, scanning the ground ahead for puddles, going as quickly as she could through the alley. It wasn't quite dark yet and images of the buildings on either side of her reflected in the water pooled on the ground. Intently focused on keeping her shoes dry, she almost bumped into a stack of wooden crates jutting into her path. She caught her footing and moved to get around it, looking up for the first time in a while, and saw a tall figure directly in front of her.

It happened fast. Before Evelyn knew it, he was behind her with one arm pinning her back to his chest and the other holding a pistol against her temple, the barrel icy against her skin. Evelyn didn't have time to scream. She didn't even know if any sound would come out if she opened her mouth. He shuffled her toward the side of the building, slamming her against the hard brick wall. He pushed her head down until she slid her back down the wall and sat on the pavement with her legs pulled up against her chest. She stayed seated as the rainwater soaked through her dress. The man, wearing a long black coat and dark hat along with a bandana wrapped around the lower half of his face, held the gun close to Evelyn as he grabbed her bag and began rifling through it. He glanced at her every few seconds as if to warn her not to try and run. She wouldn't dream of it. Her gut was telling her cooperation was the only way she was going to survive this encounter.

His gun hand was shaking slightly a few inches in front of her face, and Evelyn hoped he wouldn't accidentally pull the trigger. The very thought made her whimper, causing the man's head to snap up. Glaring, he uttered his first words to her. "Shut up, or I swear I'll kill you!"

Her anxiety rose. Her journal, still wrapped in her handkerchief, thudded to the wet ground as he threw it from her bag. She wanted badly to pick it up, but moving wasn't worth it.

Visibly impatient, the man overturned the handbag, dumping the remainder of the contents out onto the pavement. He hurriedly selected her coin purse, her jewel-encrusted compact mirror, and the pearl hairpin her mother had given her for her tenth birthday. She wanted to beg him to leave the hairpin but knew her mother would understand why she couldn't speak up right then.

After a few long, grueling moments, Evelyn's attacker stuffed the items in his coat pocket and spun on the balls of his feet to face her, the gun still in her face. He pressed the barrel to her head again, right between her eyes, firmly pinning her against the wall. "Count to ten, get your stuff, then get out of here, you hear me?" His voice was forceful.

She tried to acknowledge what he had said, but her voice was so shaky she had trouble forming actual words.

"I said, did you hear me?" He was angrier and more desperate than before.

"Yes!" Evelyn sputtered, the palms of her hands flat against the wet ground.

He stood, continuing to point the gun at her as he took several steps backward. He finally turned and sprinted down the alley, leaving her sitting in a chilly puddle surrounded by her scattered, damp belongings. She didn't count to ten. She sat in the same spot for a while until she was certain he was gone, then shakily made her way to her feet. She bent over to pick up her bag and throw her things inside, willing herself not to cry yet. Her heart was still racing, and her hands were unsteady, making it harder to get the items into her purse. She recovered her umbrella, which she had dropped when the man first startled her. She brushed rainwater off her coat and ran in the opposite direction.

Finally home and in her bedroom, Evelyn sobbed into her pillow as she replayed the scene in the alley, picturing all the different, terrifying ways it could have ended. She couldn't understand how she had been so calm and collected in the moment, but now in the safety of her own apartment, she was too afraid to turn out the lights or stray too far away from the carving knife she'd retrieved from the kitchen and placed on her nightstand.

Next to the large knife was Evelyn's dream journal with dark wet spots that marred the cover and wrinkled the pages. She was grateful to her earlier self for wrapping the journal in her handkerchief. She opened it to assess the damage. She tried not to succumb to the lump swelling in her throat as she gingerly turned each page, softly blowing on them to help dry them out. Some of her writing was smudged, and a couple of pages were slightly torn, but she was grateful she still had it. Losing a dream journal would have been devastating. It would be like losing a whole chunk of her life's memories. She picked up a pen from the nightstand and turned to the first empty page.

Her hand was still trembling slightly as she wrote carefully around the damp spots.

I am so thankful to still be here to write this. Tonight I faced what I thought was my certain death, and walking away unscathed has both humbled and terrified me. I don't know how I'll ever feel safe here again, knowing a man with a gun could be waiting for me around every corner and even in this busy city, not a soul would be there to save me. New York is the loneliest crowded place I've ever been. Tonight is the first time since I arrived here I've felt like maybe this isn't where I should be. I hope that's just the shock talking because I really do love my life here, and I'm not ready to give up everything I've worked for.

Her hand was too unsteady to go on, so Evelyn replaced the book on her nightstand, open so the pages could dry out overnight.

Her now-weathered journal reminded Evelyn that she'd started her day thinking Cole, the man in her dreams, was her biggest problem. She wasn't even sure she could get to sleep to find out what happened next with him.

She carefully placed the carving knife well within reach next to her and crawled under her covers. She spent the next several hours listening for any noises in her apartment before the weight of the day finally took over and she fell asleep.

Chapter 5
2003

Paranoia from the dream about her mugging in the alley overwhelmed Evelyn the next morning. Somehow the embarrassment of her date with Cole was a welcome distraction. She sat on the couch with her phone and folded her legs underneath her, preparing herself for her best friend's "I told you so" speech.

Cammie answered on the first ring. "Tell me everything!"

Evelyn rolled her eyes and smiled. "Let's just say you might be right about some of the things you said about Cole."

"Duh. Where'd he take you?"

"Jekyll and Hyde—" Evelyn winced as Cammie's uproarious laughter blasted through the phone into her ear.

"Wait," Cammie panted, "you're telling me he took you to a children's restaurant for your anniversary?"

"It's not just for kids!" Evelyn couldn't even say it with a straight face. "Okay, it was really bad. It was the worst. A fake rhino head on the wall hit on me during dinner and then Cole's busboy friend Matt sat at our table drinking. It's like my boyfriend doesn't know me at all."

More laughter. "Uh huh. Now tell me about the gift, because I can't wait to hear this." Cammie was enjoying this a little too much.

"Well, I'm now the proud owner of two tickets to some car show, I guess?" Evelyn readied herself for more laughter from her friend.

"Don't even think about asking me to come with you," Cammie answered between giggles.

"Oh, don't worry. It's another perfect date with Cole."

"Ev, I know we're joking around, but seriously, doesn't this bother you? How could he possibly think you would like any of that stuff? You don't have to be an Evelyn expert like me to know you don't like weird theme restaurants or loud, obnoxious cars! Don't you want to be with someone who pays attention to your likes and dislikes?"

"Yes, but I also don't know if one bad date is worth throwing away an entire relationship." Evelyn glanced at the clock. "Hey, I gotta go. I have to get ready for that party I told you about."

"That party in Brooklyn? Be careful. That's not a great part of town."

"Cole is meeting me there. Don't worry," Evelyn assured her friend.

"Okay, have fun!"

She knew Cammie was right about the neighborhood, but she was taking a cab to the party and Cole would be with her on the way home. She'd had a long couple of days in both her lives, so she was happy to let loose a little. It had been a while since she'd been to a house party, but she hoped it would be fun. Some of her friends from her poli sci classes would be there, and it was going to be a lot quieter than a bar or a club. After donning a pair of low-rise jeans and a pink one-shouldered tank top, Evelyn checked herself one last time in the mirror before heading downstairs.

An hour later, Evelyn was in the kitchen at the party, making small talk with some acquaintances. After a few minutes, another familiar face walked in, causing her stomach to do that same guilty little flip it had done in the dining hall the day before.

"Will!" Evelyn greeted him with a friendly hug. "I thought you had to study tonight!"

"I decided to come out instead of spending my Friday night writing a constitutional law paper." Will smirked, taking a soda from the fridge.

"A wise decision."

"I actually have to go in a few minutes," he said as the two found a clear spot in the kitchen where they could keep talking. "I have to get up early tomorrow."

Evelyn crossed her arms and tried to smile through her disappointment. "So, you ready for the rally on Monday?"

"I think so. We just need to pick up the signs from the printer and we'll be good to go!"

"Awesome. Thank you for all your help with this, by the way. I seriously couldn't do it without you." She meant it. He had been invaluable as they'd prepared for the rally.

"Happy to do it."

"I hope it goes well. I'm a little nervous!"

"I'm kinda excited, as weird as that sounds. I love stuff like this. Activism makes me tick. What can I say? I'm a nerd." He shrugged.

"Well, if you're a nerd, then so am I. Actually, I would be like, Head Nerd, since I'm the organizer of the rally, wouldn't I?"

"Well, now that you mention it . . ." he answered with a glint in his eye.

Evelyn laughed. A pang of guilt immediately washed over her at how much she was enjoying Will's company even knowing Cole could walk in at any second. They continued their conversation until Will finished his drink and had to leave. They hugged, and he said goodbye to the hosts of the party, classmates of theirs. Evelyn joined a group playing a game of poker around the kitchen table while she waited for Cole to arrive.

After a few hands, a loud scuffle in the living room interrupted their game. It was difficult to understand what was being said over the music playing in the background, but from what Evelyn could hear, two men were arguing over money. Shortly, one of the men involved in the confrontation threatened to come back for what was owed him before he slammed the door and left. An awkward silence hung over the house, but soon conversations picked up again and everyone went back to partying.

Evelyn returned to the game, hoping Cole would get there soon. Even if she wasn't particularly excited to see him after their date, she knew she would feel a little better with him around following the incident in the living room. After winning two hands in a row, she got into the spirit of the game and put the clash behind her.

Cole finally arrived and joined Evelyn at the poker table. She was glad she could avoid talking to him about their awful anniversary date for a while longer as they kept playing.

A few minutes later, the party was interrupted again when the front door of the house flew open with a loud bang, and three men, including the one who had previously left in anger, burst into the home, each brandishing a handgun.

Evelyn's instincts took over, and she ran for the first door she found, which happened to be to the pantry. She slid inside and tried to shut the double doors, but there wasn't enough room with her inside, so she held them together as closely as she could to make it look like they were closed. Her breath was unsteady, and her chest heaved with panic. She peeked through the slit between the doors at the chaos in the kitchen. People were screaming and running for the front door, the door to the basement, and the balcony. The gunmen were not in sight, and Evelyn trembled as she waited for the ordeal to end.

She was still holding the door tight against her body when the sound of Cole's voice made the hair on her arms stand up.

"Get out of here, man!" He was in the kitchen yelling at someone. Her stomach dropped when she saw one of the gunmen push the barrel of his weapon into Cole's chest.

A voice cried, "Don't!" It took Evelyn a second to realize the voice had been her own. Immediately the gunman and Cole both snapped their heads in her direction.

In no time, the gunman had shoved Cole to the ground and yanked Evelyn out of the pantry by her arm. He flung her to the floor, his gun pointed at her head. "Sit down!"

Cole was right behind him. "Get away from her!" He jumped on the gunman's back, causing the weapon to fall to the ground. Evelyn was too far away to reach it, and before she could move, the gunman snatched it back. He scrambled to his feet and pointed it at Cole, who was running for the living room.

The assailant chased after Cole, leaving Evelyn on the kitchen floor, quivering. She could hear more commotion in other parts of the house, but she had nowhere else to go, and her shaky legs wouldn't carry her even if she did. She crawled behind the kitchen island and sat with her back to the cabinets, holding her knees to her chest and squeezing her eyes shut, her hands over her ears. She jumped and cried out when someone touched her on the arm.

"Hey, they're gone. Are you okay?"

Evelyn looked up at one of the girls from the poker game. She nodded in response, still quaking from head to toe.

"Listen, I don't wanna freak you out, but your boyfriend did get hurt."

Evelyn's body went numb.

The girl continued. "He's okay, but I'm warning you, there's a lot of blood."

Evelyn shot up from the corner and flew to the bathroom. When she got there, she pushed her way through a small crowd gathered near the door. Splashes of red were splattered on the walls and floor. Cole was bent over the sink, blood soaking his shirt.

"Oh my God! Cole, are you okay? Has anyone called 911?"

"Yeah, I'm good. They're coming," Cole said breathily, pressing a hand towel against the wound on the left side of his skull and sucking air through his teeth in pain.

Cole was soon in an ambulance on his way to receive medical attention. Evelyn had begged to go with him, but the police refused, telling her only family could do that. They instructed Evelyn and everyone else to stick around and give witness statements about what had happened that night. By the time the whole ordeal was over, the sun was rising, and all Evelyn wanted was to go home.

Evelyn and Cole arrived at her apartment hours later, after the police had driven him back to the party house from the hospital and she was released from the scene after writing out her statement and answering questions. She tucked him into her bed and carefully put her dream journal where he couldn't see it. The exhaustion was finally kicking in, and she climbed carefully into bed next to her boyfriend, who was already asleep thanks to the pain medication.

She stared at the row of thick silver staples, wondering if she would ever be able to fall asleep again. Visions of the night's events played in her brain over and over. It was impossible for Evelyn not to let her mind wander to all the alternate endings the night could have had. She regretted inviting Cole. If she hadn't, he wouldn't be hurt right now. She was glad Will had left before the incident happened.

She scolded herself for thinking of Will while her boyfriend, who had been badly injured defending her from a gunman, was sleeping next to her with staples in his skull.

She shook her head to dismiss the thoughts and turned toward Cole. Closing her eyes, she tried to force herself to go back to her dreams, knowing things weren't much better there but exhausted and needing the rest nonetheless.

An hour later, turning over in bed again, Evelyn sighed and tossed the covers off herself. Sleep was not coming. She sat up slowly, not wanting to wake Cole. She paused to make sure he was fast asleep before she carefully slid open her nightstand drawer and retrieved her journal. She padded to the living room, where she settled on the couch and wrapped herself in a blanket to write.

All I can think about are those guns against my skin, their handlers threatening to end my life if I made one wrong move. Will that chill ever go away?

I've been avoiding admitting to myself the other part of this whole thing that's really bothering me: it happened in both of my lives only a day apart. It's as though I saw my future in my dreams, somehow. That's never happened before. I can't recall a time my dreams so closely predicted what would happen in this life. I suppose it could be a coincidence. They both seemed so utterly real it's hard to tell which one was a dream. The fear was the same in both places. The cold gunmetal on my forehead was the same. The shame of sliding my back down a wall to preserve my own life in a situation I had no control over was the same.

Are my dreams starting to predict my reality?

It was a rabbit hole Evelyn wasn't prepared to fall into so late at night, and she knew she needed sleep. Writing in her journal had helped her relax a bit, so she closed the book, slipped back into her bedroom, and put it away in her nightstand. As she got into bed next to Cole again, he stirred but didn't wake up. She softly lay down and pulled the covers over her before finally giving in to the fatigue.

Soon she was back in 1919.

Chapter 6
1919

It was Saturday, and Evelyn didn't have work, thankfully. Her head was pounding, and her jaw was throbbing. She had been clenching her teeth all night as she slept. How could she not? Gunmen were popping up in her dreams and her real life, and the dreams seemed just as real. She still hadn't told anyone about the attack last night in the alley.

She got dressed for brunch with her friends. They had been going to the diner every other Saturday at ten o'clock for as long as she could remember. They almost always sat at the same booth and almost always had the same waitress, Pearl, who knew their favorite orders by heart. The girls had shared so many laughs, tears, heartbreaks, and celebrations at that table, but she couldn't recall anyone ever having to relay a near-death experience in a back alley.

Apprehensive about leaving the apartment after her assault, Evelyn grabbed her umbrella in case she needed it for protection, though it hadn't been much help the previous day. Today she would be sure not to drop it when—*if*—anyone attacked her while she was out. She greeted her friend Edward, the elevator attendant, but her mind was elsewhere. She pushed open the doors, took a deep breath, and exhaled slowly as she walked back onto the city streets where, just a day ago, she'd believed she was safe.

Evelyn hurried to the diner. She wondered if anyone would notice her umbrella on this perfectly sunny day. She peered through the window. The girls were already seated. Emily waved excitedly, beckoning her inside. They'd already ordered her hot tea and biscuits.

Evelyn slid into the booth next to Ada and greeted the girls, her signature cheerfulness noticeably absent from her demeanor.

"Are you okay, Ev?" Lily asked, noticing her friend's tired eyes and the handle of the umbrella poking out from behind her.

Evelyn blinked away the tears that immediately formed in her eyes. She hadn't expected to get emotional so quickly. "Not exactly," she replied, sipping her hot tea. "Something really scary happened." The words stuck in her throat as she told the story aloud for the very first time.

"I was walking home from work yesterday in the rain, and—" She stopped to catch her breath, dabbing her eyes with a napkin.

Evelyn's three friends shared a concerned look, furrowing their brows in concern.

"Ev, it's okay. Take your time. Tell us what happened." Ada rubbed her friend's shoulder for encouragement.

Evelyn gulped again, her heart racing as though she were reliving the attack as she spoke. "It was raining, so I took the alley by the office, and I've never seen anyone there before, but this man, he just—" She paused, her pulse quickening. "He attacked me and held a gun to my head," she whispered.

The girls all gasped, and Emily couldn't help but let out a loud "What?!" that turned the heads of some nearby diners. When everyone got back to their meals, Emily whispered again, "What?!"

As she told her friends about the man in the alley, Evelyn's throat became dry with panic.

"So you don't know what he looked like?" asked Ada.

"Did you call the police?" Emily was wide-eyed.

"No, and no," said Evelyn. "A bandana covered his face, and afterward, all I wanted to do was go home and lock my door and hide in bed." She was still fighting tears as she replayed the memory in her head.

Lily chimed in. "Well Ev, you gotta tell the cops! Don't you want your stuff back?"

"What I want is to forget this ever happened and move on with my life." She was a little firmer than she had intended. "I'm sorry. I'm just a little on edge this morning."

"It would be weird if you *weren't* on edge!" Ada put her arm around Evelyn and pulled her close in a side hug. "Oh, Ev. I'm sorry."

Evelyn rested her head on her friend's shoulder, and for a moment wished she could leave it there and go to sleep, but her dreams were hardly more comforting.

She forced herself to sit upright and gather herself so she could eat. Exhaustion overcame her, but the thought of sleep was also stressful after the incident at the party. It annoyed her that she was afraid to sleep now, instead of being excited like before the attack. Evelyn hated the gunman in her dreams just as much as the one in the alley. Her dream life used to be her escape. She was furious that he had stolen that from her.

Emily's voice snapped Evelyn out of her thoughts as she prepared to leave the diner after their meal. "Ev, you ready?"

Evelyn gathered her bag and umbrella, and as she turned toward the door, she almost crashed into the chest of a very tall, handsome man. On any other day, it may not have startled her so much, but she was extra jumpy this morning, and she gasped loudly in fright, slapping her hand over her mouth.

"I'm so sorry. Are you all right?" He put his hand on her upper arm to steady her.

"Yes, I'm sorry. I didn't see you there!" Evelyn blushed at her own melodramatic reaction. "I startle easily. You're lucky I didn't impale you with my umbrella!"

"I would be very unlucky indeed to be attacked by the only umbrella being carried in Manhattan on the most beautiful day of the year," he quipped, straining his neck to see the clear blue sky through the diner window.

"You've got me there," she said, letting her guard down a bit.

"Ev, you gonna introduce us to your friend?" asked Ada.

The man made direct eye contact with Evelyn, smiling as he answered. "I'm Calvin."

Chapter 7
1919

His friends called him Cal, but he hated it. He was an investment banker who had moved to the city five years ago from Connecticut to work on Wall Street with the big boys. He had a deep, soothing voice, and when he looked at Evelyn, she became helplessly attentive. As he walked her to her building from the diner, the two got to know each other better. Evelyn almost forgot Ada and Lily were walking behind them, monitoring the proceedings. Emily had plans to visit her sister that afternoon, so she had left the diner separately, but not before insisting on a full update about the walk home as soon as possible. The girls would never let her leave the diner alone with a man she didn't know, especially after the alley. She was grateful for her friends here in the city. Without them, the only person she could really count on was Mr. Allen, and she wasn't comfortable telling him about her brush with the gunman.

Evelyn and Calvin chatted intently. He was confident. His gait was sure and his stride steady. They were approaching the door to her apartment building, and Evelyn was running out of time to get Calvin to commit to ever speaking to her again.

As if reading her mind, he stopped and faced her.

"Forgive me if I'm being presumptuous, but can I see you again?"

Smiling bashfully, Evelyn nodded. "Of course! When?"

"What are you doing tomorrow afternoon?" he replied without skipping a beat.

Evelyn raised her eyebrows, impressed at his tenacity. "Nothing. Yet."

"Meet me right here at two o'clock."

"It's a plan." Evelyn glanced at her friends who were pretending not to eavesdrop and doing a poor job of it.

Calvin said his goodbyes to Ada and Lily, then took her right hand and politely kissed it. "Until tomorrow, Ms. Moore."

"Two o'clock," she said, her cheeks warming.

He nodded, turned, and walked away.

Evelyn and her friends made sure he was out of sight before squealing and laughing. Ada and Lily agreed Calvin was a major catch for Evelyn. Thanking her friends for walking her home and for their support, Evelyn said her goodbyes and went inside. For almost a block and a half, she had forgotten about the alley. She balled her fists in anger upon remembering it. One thing was for sure: the man in the alley was *not* going to ruin the man in the diner.

Evelyn had no plans for the rest of the day, so she locked her door, checking it several times to make sure it was fast. Still exhausted, she flopped down on her bed with the latest copy of *Harper's Bazaar*. Only a few minutes into flipping through the pages, drowsiness came over her. Not surprised given everything that had happened in the last twenty-four hours, Evelyn allowed herself to drift off. She'd meant to write in her journal about Calvin, but she was too tired. She would do it in the morning.

Chapter 8
2003

Blood stained the water light red as Evelyn wrung Cole's shirt from the party into the bathtub. She worked to get as much of it out of Cole's collared shirt as she could. The sight of it brought back memories of the night before. The wall. Cole's head with metal staples holding a gaping gash together.

She had been so mad at him just yesterday for ruining their anniversary and proving he hadn't been paying attention to any of her likes and dislikes for a year, and twenty-four hours later she couldn't help but think she owed him her life. The man had literally proven he would take a bullet for her. It had to mean *something*.

Her mind raced as she went over the party, the guns, Cole, and the rally she still needed to oversee. She also contemplated her dreams, where she had been attacked in much the same way she had here. To take her mind off everything, she thought about Calvin. Hardly noticing the corners of her lips curling up in a smile as she wondered where her dream date would take her, she glimpsed herself in the bathroom mirror and cleared her throat, bringing herself back to reality where she was currently hanging up her boyfriend's bloody shirt from the time he'd jumped in front of a gun to protect her.

"Hey, I gotta go down to the police station since I didn't give my witness statement last night," Cole said, poking his head into the bathroom.

She moved toward him, lifting her hand to turn his head slightly to inspect his stapled wound. "Are you sure you're okay to go on your own? I can go to the printer later to get the rally signs if you want me to go with you."

"I'm good, I promise." He tousled her hair playfully as though she were a child. She always hated it when he did that, but under the circumstances, she let it slide.

Wiping the hair back from her eyes, she studied the face of the man who had risked his life for her the night before. She debated whether, in light of what had happened, she owed Cole forgiveness for his thoughtless gifts and disregard for her preferences. They hugged briefly and kissed goodbye, and Cole left. She locked the door firmly behind him and busied herself getting ready to go to the printer to pick up her signs.

About forty-five minutes later, Evelyn almost crashed into a familiar figure on her way into the print shop. "Will!"

"Hey! Didn't you get my IM?" He greeted her with a quick hug. "I said I'd pick up the signs. I figured after what happened at the party last night, you might need today to rest and take care of Cole."

She slapped her hand to her forehead. "Oh, I didn't even check my IMs. I'm so sorry. Thank you. I've been such a mess since last night."

"Yeah, our friends told me. Sounds like it got intense pretty fast," Will said. "I guess I left just in time."

She scoffed. "You have no idea."

"I heard Cole got hurt. Is he okay?" He put the rally signs down on the sidewalk next to him.

"He's got a head full of giant staples and my bathtub looks like a murder scene, but I guess other than that, he's good. I just wish he hadn't gotten there when he did. Or that I had taken your lead and left earlier."

"Don't blame yourself. You couldn't have known that was going to happen. I'm sorry. I feel bad that I left you there to deal with all that on your own." He put his hand on her shoulder, then quickly removed it when he realized what he was doing.

"Don't apologize!" Evelyn was eager to change the subject. "Hey, you wanna go grab some coffee?" She pointed to a coffee shop across the street.

"Uh, sure," Will said, checking his phone for the time. He smiled at her. "I don't have to be anywhere for a while."

Taking a few of the rally signs from him, Evelyn walked toward the coffee shop with Will. She tried to think of something clever to say, but her brain was like mush. She couldn't tell if it was because she was so tired from the last couple of days or because he was giving her those butterflies she would never admit to having. Eventually she blurted out, "So, are you dating anyone?" She probably shouldn't have asked, but she was admittedly curious.

Will chuckled. "No. You may have noticed I'm kind of shy. I don't tend to be much of a lady's man."

"That's actually a huge plus these days. It's refreshing to talk to a guy who would take time out of his Saturday afternoon to pick up signs at the printer for a political protest."

"Wow, don't make me sound like such a dork!" He laughed, holding the door to the coffee place open.

"Excuse me, we already talked about this, remember? I like nerds!" Evelyn reminded herself not to cross the line into flirtation. She didn't want to appear as though she was leading Will on. She had a boyfriend, after all. One who had made himself a hero the night before. She would keep things platonic with Will.

The two found a table and put the signs underneath it. As Will stood in line to order their drinks, Evelyn wondered if he'd ever had a serious girlfriend. She couldn't imagine him trying to hit on anyone, but she could definitely understand how someone would want him as a boyfriend. He seemed like the relationship type—another thing they had in common. She might have much more in common with Will than she did with Cole, but she couldn't imagine Will would get into a gunman's face to defend her. Would he? Evelyn was deep in thought when he got back to the table with their drinks.

He placed her hot tea in front of her and sat across from her at the small table next to the window. They began chatting as pedestrians strolled by on the sidewalk outside.

The more they talked, the more Evelyn enjoyed Will's company. They had never been alone together before, and the conversation flowed easily. She didn't have to force herself to stick to certain topics to keep Will's interest like she often did with Cole. Will told her all about his family and his aspirations to work at the United Nations someday. He said it was one reason he was so excited to hold the rally there. The office he wanted to work for, the UN Development Programme, focused on eliminating poverty in impoverished nations. Evelyn admired his selfless choice and couldn't help but warm to him more upon learning about his career goals and his desire to make a difference in the world. She could relate.

What she meant to be a quick stop for coffee turned into an hour-long banter that had them both entranced.

Evelyn glanced at the time on her phone and realized how late it was. "Oh, no. Cole will be back from giving his statement soon. I've gotta get going. I'm sorry."

"I should get home, too." Will stood to gather the signs and his phone. "I really do hope Cole is okay. And you."

"I will be. I just need to process, I think."

"Well, I'm here if you need to talk it out," Will said. "Actually, all I have is your email and your screen name. Lemme give you my number so you can text me if you need. And so we can find each other at the rally."

There it was. The Will-induced stomach flip. "Oh, yeah, good call!" She handed him her phone and tried to play it cool, taking his and typing her number in as well. Once they had their own phones back, he gathered the signs again.

On the sidewalk, they determined they were headed in different directions. Will almost bid Evelyn goodbye but quickly thought better of it. "Hey, I know it might be a little scary walking around the city alone after what happened last night. Do you want me to walk with you to the subway or get you a cab?"

If Cole caught her with Will, she would never hear the end of it, but she was skittish about going home alone, so she took him up on his offer to get her a cab.

When one pulled up, Will opened the door and reached in, handing the driver a twenty-dollar bill. "Get her home safely? Thanks."

The driver nodded.

Evelyn was touched. She hadn't expected him to pay for the ride. The two hugged goodbye and parted ways. "See you Monday at the rally!" she called through the open window as the cab pulled off.

"Stay safe, Evelyn!"

She smiled as the cab drove away. His genuine care warmed her heart. Maybe she couldn't picture him jumping in front of a deadly weapon for her, but he was kind and thoughtful and paid attention to her needs and interests. It had been a while since she sat down and had a real, intellectual, witty conversation with a man that left her wanting more.

The connection she had with Cole was different. It was strong but in a more animalistic way. Their bond wasn't only physical; they shared some common interests and had fun together. But there was something missing. He didn't care about the things she was most passionate about. He didn't understand why she loved watching the news or engaging in activism, and he had little to no knowledge of current events. The two were different in a lot of important ways, and Evelyn had spent a year trying to overlook them. She had been almost ready to give up on Cole completely after their anniversary date, but his actions last night at the party had softened her toward him again.

Evelyn turned her attention to the present, where Cole would soon be home from the police station and she would need to focus on taking care of her injured boyfriend.

The cab pulled up near her building, and she got out, thanking the driver. As she fumbled for her keys in her bag, a small silver sedan pulled up in front of the main door to the building and double parked. The hazard lights flashed as the passenger door opened and a man emerged from the car. She immediately recognized her boyfriend as he stepped onto the street, bending over to say goodbye to whoever was in the driver's seat. Evelyn kept her distance as Cole walked inside. She stopped on the sidewalk, pretending to check her phone while the silver car drove past her. When she got a glimpse of the driver's face, Evelyn's stomach tightened and her adrenaline instantly surged.

Anger took over, and she couldn't help but blurt out, "Are you kidding me?!"

Chapter 9
2003

Fuming, Evelyn threw open the door and marched into the lobby. Cole had already taken the elevator to her floor, she guessed, eyeing the numbers above the doors lighting up one by one. It stopped on her floor, number eight, and after an excruciatingly long wait, they finally began descending back toward the ground floor where she was waiting, clenching her jaw in fury. Frantically pushing the button for her floor again and again, she tried in vain to hurry the process along.

She burst into the apartment. Cole was standing in the kitchen in front of the open fridge. He smiled cheerfully as he greeted her. "Hey, babe!" He pulled out a bottle of Miller Light and twisted off the cap.

"Who just dropped you off?" Evelyn snapped, grabbing the bottle cap he had carelessly placed on the kitchen counter and slamming it into the garbage can.

"What are you talking about?" He took a swig from the bottle.

Her anger rose at his attempt to play dumb, and she took a deep breath before responding. "I'm pretty sure I just saw your ex-girlfriend, Alicia, dropping you off outside my building, Cole. Am I wrong?"

He pushed past her, bringing his beer into the living room, and sat on the couch. "No, you are not wrong," he said flatly. He was purposely downplaying the situation, which further infuriated Evelyn.

"Why did she drop you off? I thought you were going to the police station. Is that who drove you there?" She was firing off questions without pausing, but she was pissed, and she didn't care.

"No, I took a cab." He was way too calm.

He leaned back on the couch, beer in hand. The way he played it cool during their arguments always made her blood boil. Not because she wanted a fight, but because she wanted him to care, and he was intent on appearing as though he didn't. His passion always seemed to appear and disappear at his convenience. When he knew it would irk her, he pretended to be unaffected, and she admittedly fell for it every time. He knew how to push her buttons better than anyone she'd ever met. It was what ignited their relationship and simultaneously threatened to ruin it.

"Cole, explain to me why Alicia dropped you off!" She stood over him, trying to get his full attention.

"Because I needed a ride home," he said matter-of-factly.

She straightened, exhaling long and hard before speaking again. "Uh huh. I understand that you needed a ride home. I guess I'm just wondering why you didn't call literally *anyone* else. You know how I feel about her!"

"Well, you don't have a car, so I couldn't call *you*!" he fired back, taking another drink from the bottle.

"Should you even be drinking? You have a three-inch gash in your skull. Don't you think maybe you should *not* thin your blood?"

"Okay, Mom," he sneered, not putting the bottle down.

By now Evelyn was irate. "I can't do this. I'm really sorry you're injured, but I don't understand why you had to call her for a ride! It's so hard to trust you when you do stuff like this, Cole!"

He stood and went into the kitchen, pouring the rest of his beer into the sink. He picked up his backpack from the hallway floor and put his hand on the doorknob.

"What are you doing?"

"I'm leaving." He opened the door.

"Are you serious?"

"You don't trust me, and you're being crazy, so I'm gonna go hang somewhere else tonight," he barked, standing in the doorway facing her. She was still in the living room, glad there were several feet between them because she was seething.

"You're a huge baby, you know that?" she yelled, making her way toward the door. "And I am not being crazy. I'm catching you in another lie, and every time I do, it's with *her*!" She had reached the doorway by now, but he was already headed down the hall.

Cole didn't even look at her as he stretched his left arm back and raised his middle finger.

She went inside, slamming the door shut and letting out a furious groan as she locked it and retreated to her bedroom.

She almost turned on *Sex and the City*, which usually took her mind off her problems, but she didn't feel like watching clueless men misunderstand women on television when she had quite enough of that in her own life. Instead, she sat down on her bed and took out her dream journal. Evelyn calmed down and distracted herself by writing about Calvin. She had meant to write about meeting him all day but hadn't had time, and she wanted to get it all on paper before she forgot any details.

Cole and I just got into one of our biggest fights yet. He went to the police station today to give his statement about the night of the party, and I caught him getting a ride home from Alicia. The same Alicia he cheated on me with when we first started dating. When Cole still supposedly thought we "weren't official yet." Alicia seems to keep popping up in his life every few weeks, and it's becoming harder and harder to believe his smug excuses.

On a happier note, I met someone very intriguing in my dream last night. Calvin is a successful, handsome, confident businessman who appeared to hang on to my every word as we talked. We are going out together again soon, and I can't wait to see where it goes. If I can't have a good boyfriend in this life, maybe I can at least have one in my dreams?

I should mention the other thing that's bugging me. Meeting Calvin was another similarity between my dreams and my waking life. I was held at gunpoint in both, and the very next day I bumped into a man in both lives who I am not dating but who have caught my attention. Cole and Will are polar opposites, and from what I can tell, Will isn't trying to date me, so maybe it's not exactly *the same, but I can't help noticing the parallels between my two worlds recently. It's a little eerie.*

One thing I can be relatively sure of, though, is that Calvin's date will surely outdo Cole's anniversary date!

Evelyn put the pen down and buried herself under the covers fully clothed. She turned the pages in the journal back to some of her favorite dreams. She often did this when she wanted to fall asleep, but only when Cole wasn't around. He'd made it clear he didn't like her dream journal because she didn't want him to read it. He couldn't stand the idea of her having secrets from him, though she'd never given him any reason to mistrust her. It was yet another red flag from Cole she had chosen to ignore.

The words on the page grew fuzzy as the comfort of her bed won her over, and soon she succumbed to the coziness and was on her way back to her dreams.

Chapter 10
1919

Evelyn couldn't help her giddiness as she checked herself in the mirror one more time, making sure everything was perfect for her date with Calvin. He was unexpected in her life, and she was impressed with her own confidence in saying yes to a man she barely knew. It wasn't like her, but after her close call in the alley, she thought saying yes to more things in life might not be a bad idea. She especially needed the distraction after Cole had left her so enraged in her dreams. Again.

She wrapped her coat around her shoulders and exited her apartment, making her way downstairs to meet Calvin. She was a little early, but she didn't want to keep him waiting. To her surprise, when the elevator doors opened, he was already standing in the lobby. He flashed a winning grin as he walked toward her.

"Good afternoon." She greeted him happily.

"Ms. Moore, a pleasure." He opened the door for her and led her to the sidewalk. "I hope you don't mind my being a few minutes early."

"Not at all! And please, call me Evelyn. Where are we going?" she asked as she climbed into the car he had waiting.

"Can't tell you. It'd ruin the surprise!"

About fifteen minutes later, the car pulled up outside a tall building on Broadway. Calvin opened the car door once again. As soon as Evelyn stepped out of the car, she recognized where they were.

"Is this the Woolworth Building?"

"The one and only." He offered his arm, and the two entered the lobby of the regal edifice, a doorman holding the elaborate doors. She gasped, taking in the ornate space with its fabulous arches and columns that reached up to the high ceiling. It was breathtaking.

"It's something, isn't it?" Calvin said, leading her down a grand staircase toward the elevator doors. "Wait 'til you get to the top!"

An elevator attendant in a formal uniform opened the doors for them, and Calvin allowed her inside first. "Take it away, Doug." Calvin was obviously familiar with the attendant.

Evelyn had no idea how Calvin knew anyone here, but she was excited to tour the magnificent building and felt important on the arm of this handsome, evidently well-connected man. The elevator doors finally opened on the fifty-seventh floor, revealing the most spectacular view of New York Evelyn had ever seen.

Her mouth agape, Evelyn laughed in wonder as she surveyed her beloved city from a height she had never experienced. She'd heard of the Woolworth Observation Deck but never thought she would actually get to go there. Calvin walked up next to her as she took in the view, and she couldn't help but grab his arm with both hands in excitement. She tugged his arm, imploring him to look at the sights from another angle. "Show me the rest!"

A handful of other sightseers milled about, but Evelyn hardly noticed them. Calvin showed her around the entire observation deck, pointing out city landmarks and interesting sites. He could have made it all up, but Evelyn didn't care. She was dumbstruck.

After touring the deck and getting a full view of New York from the tallest building in the city, Evelyn couldn't imagine what Calvin had planned next. She expected they would return to the lobby, but to her surprise, Doug stopped the elevator on another floor. Calvin stepped out and offered his hand to help her off.

"What's on this floor?" Evelyn asked, perplexed. There were office doors and windows lining the hallway, but she couldn't guess what they were doing here on a date.

"Follow me." He took a set of keys from his pocket.

She followed him a few dozen feet until he stopped at a wooden door with a plaque on it for an accounting firm. Even more confused, Evelyn wondered if she should go inside. She didn't really know Calvin, after all.

Sensing her hesitation, Calvin assured her. "It's nothing odd. Trust me."

"Okay." She was amused but unsure.

Calvin led her down another smaller hallway and opened the doors to a luxurious conference room with a commanding view of the city through a large window. A small picnic lunch was set up at one end of the large wooden conference table, with two chairs next to one another. Pulling one out, he beckoned for her to sit down.

"You set this up?" An office picnic wasn't exactly what she'd imagined for the day, but the view was unbeatable, and the idea was so original that Evelyn couldn't help but get swept up in the romance of it all. The two chatted and got to know each other better as they nibbled on cheese and grapes and sipped champagne that he topped off as needed. He was smooth, and she wondered how many other women he had given this treatment to before her. She almost asked but, not wanting to ruin this day for herself, refrained. There were stark differences between this date and Cole's epic flop the other night.

Soon, Evelyn was telling Calvin about the man in the alley. She didn't know if it was his personality or the champagne that made her comfortable enough to tell him, but she found herself unable to keep from pouring the story out to this man she barely knew. When she finished speaking, he sat wide-eyed in the chair next to her.

"I am so sorry that happened to you," he said earnestly. After a brief pause, he added, "Vulnerable women really shouldn't be in dark alleys alone, you know." He reached for the champagne bottle and refilled both their glasses. "To your safety." He raised his glass in a toast.

"My safety." She clinked her glass against his, unsure of what to make of his attempt at helpful advice. Her instinct was to give him a rundown of why his words were offensive, but she didn't want to ruin the afternoon. Aside from the strange comment, the day was perfect. Evelyn focused her attention fully back onto Calvin, who had already moved on to another topic. She willfully ignored the tiny voice inside her head telling her it was all too good to be true and allowed herself to enjoy the date.

Chapter 11
1919

Evelyn and Calvin talked and laughed so much the hours flew by. The bottle of champagne was long gone. Much better acquainted as the bubbles dampened their inhibitions, they were laughing at his latest joke when he stood up from his chair and walked toward the large window overlooking City Hall Park and the west side of Manhattan. "Beautiful sunset from here." He glanced back at her over his shoulder. "Wanna wait around and watch?"

She joined him and beamed as she took in the gorgeous view once again. "Shouldn't we go soon? It's not proper for us to be here alone after dark." She coyly nudged him with her shoulder.

"I promise, it's worth it!" He put his arm around her and pulled her closer. He checked his watch. "In about five minutes, the sky is going to change color. You'll see."

"How could you possibly know that?"

"Trust me."

The two stood chatting by the window, awaiting the sunset over the city. Just like clockwork in exactly five minutes, the sky went from a hazy blue to a pink and yellow swirl that painted the horizon like watercolors. "You're too perfect. There must be some sort of catch with you."

He chuckled. "I'm glad you're here, Evelyn." He gazed down at her. Without thinking, she raised herself up on her toes and kissed him. In a split second, he kissed her back. Pulling away after a few seconds to catch her breath, Evelyn smiled shyly and tucked her hair behind her ear.

"I wasn't planning on doing that." She laughed. "I'm sorry."

"I told you I was glad you're here!" He flashed a cheeky smile. "We should go, though. My accounting friend asked me to lock up by seven o'clock."

The two gathered the picnic supplies and empty champagne bottle, placing them in a wicker basket in a corner of the room. "Someone will come and get this tonight, don't worry," he said, leaving the basket on the table. On the elevator down to the beautiful lobby, Evelyn was on cloud nine. She never wanted this date to end.

Outside, she shuddered slightly at the uncharacteristic chill of the September evening. Calvin offered her his coat, wrapping it around her shoulders.

"I'll get you safely home. Then unfortunately I have to meet up with some friends from the firm. Shop talk."

Trying to hide her disappointment, Evelyn lied. "Oh, of course! I need to get home, too. I have plans early tomorrow morning." She hoped she wasn't blushing too much.

"I would love to go out with you again, Ms. Moore," he said, looking down at her.

"I would like that as well, Mr.—" She paused, realizing she didn't even know his last name. Now she was definitely blushing.

"Nelson," he interjected with a smile, noticing her embarrassment.

"Mr. Nelson." She grinned. The two shared a taxi, chatting and flirting all the way to her apartment. Evelyn was sad the date was ending but couldn't believe her luck and the day she'd just had. She couldn't let him leave before finishing their conversation about plans for another date, and she racked her brain to think of an upcoming event she could invite him to without sounding too desperate.

Before she could open her mouth to speak, Calvin was already taking the lead.

"Can I take you out on Wednesday evening?"

"I would like that very much." She couldn't hide her smile.

"I'll pick you up after work?"

"It's a date."

The car pulled up to her building. Evelyn pursed her lips, trying not to squeal in excitement as he jumped out of the car to open her door. Stepping onto the curb, she wondered if he would kiss her again here, in public. It was dark, after all, and there weren't that many people nearby.

As if reading her mind, Calvin tilted her head up with his fingers lightly under her chin and gave her a peck. She had hoped for more, but she would take this as a win.

"Goodnight, Evelyn." He cradled her hands in his.

"Goodnight," she murmured, turning to walk into the building. Evelyn forced herself to keep a straight face as she entered the lobby and headed toward the elevator. Once in the safety of her own apartment, she locked the door behind her, dropping her bag onto the floor and twirling her way into the living room, hands in the air, celebrating the absolute dream of a date she'd just had.

Speaking out loud to herself, Evelyn walked to the kitchen to pour herself a celebratory drink. "Not bad if I do say so myself, Evelyn Claire Moore!"

She took her glass into the bathroom and ran a hot bath for herself, lighting a few candles and adding some bubbles for extra luxury. She'd had such an amazing time and wasn't ready for it to end. Lowering herself into the bathtub, she rested her head on the wall behind her and closed her eyes. She sighed, smiling to herself as she thought how different this date had been from the one before. Yesterday she had woken up a paranoid, bumbling mess, unsure whether she would ever be safe again after a terrifying attack in a wet alleyway. Today she was traipsing around New York City's tallest building, having exclusive picnic lunches over a sunset skyline, and kissing a man who had connections to the Woolworth Building.

She sank lower into the tub, her hair gently tickling her back as it swayed in the water, and closed her eyes. She thought about her day with Calvin, and soon, in spite of not wanting to sleep, everything faded to black as the warmth of the water and the wine in her blood sent her off to her problems with Cole.

Chapter 12
2003

Waking up for class on Monday was bittersweet. It was the day of the rally, and as important as it was, she didn't want to leave her dreams where things were going so well with Calvin. She wanted to know what was going to happen next with him. But, though she would never admit it out loud, she was also excited to spend time with Will. He would be a welcome sight after everything that had happened with Cole. Evelyn had spent much of Sunday pondering how to proceed with Cole but promised herself she'd put him aside for the day so she could focus on the rally.

During class, she took out her journal and recounted every detail she could remember of her date with Calvin from last night's dream. It was like she was writing a scene from a movie, and she wondered why her real-life boyfriend couldn't deliver even a fraction of the romance.

Arriving outside the United Nations building that afternoon, Evelyn had no trouble finding Will. She was disappointed there weren't many people around and feared the protest wouldn't make any difference at all if no one was there to see it. Slightly worried about a possible failed event, she approached Will, who waved happily as he turned and recognized her.

"Hey!" He gave her a quick hug. "I have everything over here. We're still waiting on a few people."

"Hi! Thanks for bringing the signs." She placed her backpack on the ground. "Hey, if this goes well, maybe someone in the UN development office will see you from their window and hire you on the spot!" she joked, remembering his dream job.

He chuckled, craning his neck to look at the tall building. "I had my resume printed on one of the signs, just in case." Evelyn laughed out loud at his retort. They walked to the pile of rally supplies. Will continued more seriously. "So how are you doing, you know, after the whole gun thing at the party?"

She hadn't been expecting that question. In fact, she'd been so preoccupied thinking about Calvin and her dream date that she hadn't even given any thought to the gun incident, which was a welcome relief now that she was aware of it. "Better, actually," she replied, picking up a sign and inspecting it.

"I'm glad," he said, gathering up a few more signs as he spoke.

"I've been trying not to think about it too much."

"Sorry!" he said quickly. "I didn't mean to bring it up if you don't wanna talk about it."

"No, it's fine!" She put her hand on his forearm. "You're totally okay. I just meant I'm trying not to obsess over it." She changed the subject. "You ready to protest in front of absolutely no one?!" She motioned to the lack of spectators.

"Let's protest the heck out of this war to these . . . four people!"

The two handed out signs to the rest of the group, with more members arriving shortly after. Soon there were about eleven protesters from various colleges in the area. As the afternoon progressed, more joined, and eventually the rally was a full-blown event. By law, demonstrators outside the UN building were not allowed to march but were required to conduct a stationery protest. They waved their signs, handing out leaflets they had printed to passersby, who mostly accepted them graciously. A few responded by politely refusing the pamphlets, and two or three crumpled them up and tossed them to the ground, yelling obscenities and pro-war slogans at the protesters.

Will and Evelyn managed the event in tandem, ensuring information about the anti-war movement made its way into the hands of as many people as possible and signing more supporters up for their email list. There was a CAN convention coming up in November, and they wanted to get as many people on board as they could before then. A couple of news crews had come out to cover the protest. It wasn't the spectacle Will and Evelyn had hoped for but was overall a successful event.

Working with Will was effortless and natural for Evelyn. She didn't have to ask for the things she needed. She turned around and he was always there, one step ahead, anticipating. As she watched him talk to the public about anti-war efforts, she couldn't help but be drawn to how endearing his passion for the cause was. Cole would never do anything like this, not even for anything he cared about. He was too concerned with his image.

Alongside Will, Evelyn was happier than she had been in weeks. Being with someone who was sweet, compassionate, and cared about the same things she did was something she'd been missing, both in her dreams and her waking life. The two playfully quizzed each other on the various world flags that flew around them, each trying to stump the other with one that was impossible to recognize. Evelyn had to admit, he knew more about flags than she did, but it didn't bother her at all because he never gloated or made her feel small. She wasn't used to that. Cole was a sore loser and had broken several video game controllers, flinging them across the room in a rage after a defeat.

When the protest ended, they thanked their group members and congratulated them on a successful afternoon. Soon, the two were alone with a pile of protest signs and a box of leftover pamphlets outside the United Nations building as the sun began to set. When it was time to leave, Will seemed hesitant to part ways.

He looked up at the dusky sky. "It's getting dark. Can I walk you to the subway or get you a cab?"

Her stomach flipped. Cole would react horribly if he saw her arriving home in a cab with another guy, especially after she'd gotten so angry about Alicia driving him home, but she couldn't carry all these signs home on the subway alone. More importantly, Evelyn had never cheated on Cole, or anyone else, and he had no right to be angry. He probably wouldn't be around when she got home, anyway. She hadn't heard from him since he'd walked out of her apartment and flipped her the bird.

"Sure," she answered. "Wanna share a cab?"

The pair hailed a taxi, shoving the protest signs into the back seat before climbing in after them. Her entire body warmed with Will's thigh against hers.

"I really want to stop and get some food, but I have a paper to write."

"I wish!" He pushed the signs away from his face. "I have an outline due in the morning that I haven't even started."

"Some other time." Her voice fell.

"Soon, hopefully." Will smiled as the cab pulled up to her apartment building.

She leaned over and hugged him goodbye. He smelled good. For some reason, she hadn't expected him to be a cologne person. She didn't recognize the scent, but she liked it.

Will said goodbye to her as she closed the car door, refusing the cab fare Evelyn tried to hand him. She watched the car drive off before turning to walk inside, grinning to herself as she spun on her heel to go into the building. Her heart stopped when she noticed who was standing a few feet away.

Cole glared at her with his hands in his pockets, leaning against the wall next to the building entrance. He straightened up and came toward her. Her heart rate quickened. This was going to be bad.

"You couldn't even wait twenty-four hours before messing around with someone else?" His voice sent chills down her spine. She hated it when he got jealous. It was his least desirable trait and the one that brought out his worst temper.

"I'm not messing around, Cole." Her back stiffened in defense. "He's my classmate, and we were at the Iraq War protest today. I told you about it."

"Really? And do all your 'classmates' make you smile like that when they drop you off?"

"Come on, are you kidding me right now?" Evelyn glanced around, embarrassed that people could hear them. She led him a few feet down the sidewalk away from the building entrance where they could speak more privately.

"No, I'm not kidding," he said condescendingly. "I'm not allowed to have Alicia drop me off at your building, but you're allowed to have some random guy I don't even know drop you off after you've been doing whatever you were doing with him, and then grinning from ear to ear like you're in love with him?" He was almost yelling at this point.

"I'm not in love with him, Cole!" She tried not to raise her voice in an attempt to get him to lower his. "Will is my friend! And you and Alicia have a history of betraying me, if you recall. It's not the same!"

"Oh, now he's your friend?" He was yelling. "A second ago he was just a classmate! You wouldn't have to change your story every five seconds if you weren't lying to me!"

Evelyn clenched her jaw and balled her fists so tight her fingernails dug into her palms. She gathered what composure she could muster and took a deep breath before speaking. "Cole, I'm going inside now, and I would appreciate it if you didn't follow me. I think we need some time to cool off before we can talk about this."

"Wow," he said. "We're done."

"We're *done*?"

"Yeah, we're done. I don't wanna be with someone who cheats on me."

Before she knew what she was doing, she was crying and grabbing his arm trying not to let him walk away.

"Just come inside and we'll talk, okay?" she pleaded through tears. She hated how he always seemed to reduce her to begging.

Soon the two were in Evelyn's apartment. She locked the door behind her and sat on the living room couch, putting her head in her hands. Cole plopped down on the armchair near her, leaning forward with his elbows on his knees, ready for a fight.

"Cole, I really need you to believe me. There is nothing going on between Will and me."

"Then why were you smiling like that when you got out of that car?" he fired back.

"I don't know, he's funny!"

Somehow that angered Cole even more. Standing, he picked up a throw pillow from the armchair he had been sitting on and held it in one hand while he pummeled it with the other.

Evelyn jumped.

Cole raised the throw pillow in the air and hurled it as hard as he could in her direction.

She flinched, bracing for impact. He'd barely missed hitting her in the face with it. Her adrenaline was racing, and her mouth was dry. He was coming toward her, so she moved around the coffee table and headed for the bedroom door, trying to dodge him. Before she could get to the doorway, he cut her off.

Face to face, they stood in silence for a few excruciating moments. Soon, in a low, chillingly calm voice that made her fight-or-flight response tingle, he put his face close to hers and said, "Tell me the truth or I swear to God, I will kill him."

"What is wrong with you?" She stepped away from him, bumping into the armchair.

He advanced closer, towering over her until her back was pinned to the wall, then slowly and deliberately, he raised his hand to her throat, wrapping his fingers around it. "Tell me what happened so I know what to do to him and to you." His voice was quiet and menacingly calm. He tilted her chin up with his other hand and forced her to look him in the eye.

She had never seen him like this.

Evelyn swallowed and whispered, "Nothing happened. There's nothing going on between us, Cole, I swear. He's just a guy from class."

He shoved her up against the wall with the hand holding her throat. She sputtered for air at the impact.

Suddenly, he let her go and turned away. She exhaled sharply and regained her breath. Unsure of what he would do next, she ran into her bedroom, slamming the door shut and locking it. She leaned her body against the door and yelled shakily, "Cole, please leave! You're scaring me!" Panting and trying not to cry, she listened carefully for him to approach. Instead, she heard the apartment door slam shut.

She waited a while before making any moves. Gathering her strength, she finally called out, "Cole?"

There was no answer. She carefully stood up, her legs unsteady, and unlocked the bedroom door. She peeked out to make sure he was gone. Satisfied he had left, she rushed to the apartment door and locked the deadbolt. Back in the living room, she retrieved the pillow Cole had thrown at her. She hugged it close as she melted into the couch, sobbing.

Chapter 13
1919

Evelyn's feet were dragging when she got to the office. She'd slapped on a bit of makeup and thrown her hair back that morning, and her outfit wasn't perfectly pressed, as it usually was. From the high of her perfect date with Calvin to the absolute low of Cole putting his hands on her, her head was all over the place. Cole had left her so uneasy it had followed her into this life. Sometimes it was difficult compartmentalizing what happened in one world versus the other.

She placed her bag on her desk, and as she settled in her chair, Evelyn replayed the altercation in her mind for what was probably the hundredth time that morning. Cole's rage-filled eyes inches from hers as he pinned her against the wall by her throat. Without thought, she reached up and ran her fingers over where he'd gripped her, almost expecting a bruise or some tenderness. But, she reminded herself again, it had been a dream. A nightmare, really.

"Ah! You're early!" said Mr. Allen cheerfully as he entered the room from his office, startling Evelyn out of her thoughts. "How was your weekend?" He placed some paperwork in the inbox at the corner of her desk.

"It was—" Evelyn paused, almost blurting out her story about Cole, then remembering her real-life date with Calvin. "It was actually great!" She surprised herself as she remembered that something truly magical had also happened over the weekend.

"Glad to hear it!" Mr. Allen said. "By the way, I have a lunch meeting with Wilson today, so if you don't mind staying around and watching the office in case anyone comes in . . ." He trailed off.

"No problem!" Mr. Allen turned and walked back into his office, shouting his thanks over his shoulder as he went. Picking up the papers in her inbox, Evelyn got to work. She couldn't admit it to her boss, but she was uneasy about being alone so close to where she'd been attacked.

She found the typing and filing to be an effective distraction from thinking about the mugging or Cole. The more she threw herself into her work, the less she thought about any of it, and before she knew it, it was lunchtime.

Mr. Allen emerged in his hat and coat, ready for his meeting. Evelyn had almost forgotten he was going out.

"See you later!" She waved as he exited.

Peeking in before closing the door behind him, Mr. Allen replied, "Back in a bit, dear."

The door clicked, ushering in the heaviness of the silence around her, and her breathing became shallow with fright. It was the first time she'd been by herself here since the attack, and she couldn't help but wonder whether the gunman knew where she worked and if he would come back.

She stood and rushed to the door and locked it, sure to click the deadbolt into place. Annoyed with herself for still being so afraid after the alley and everything that had been happening in her dreams, she made her way back to her desk and pulled her journal out of her bag. She wrote hurriedly. The emotions were pumping through her blood, and she wanted to get them out onto paper. To distract herself from the gunman and how scared she was at present, Evelyn scribbled down the story of what Cole had done to her.

Cole has never put his hands on me before. I've seen him get jealous, but I never thought it would go this far. For the first time, I was scared of him. Not scared of fighting with him but scared of him. I don't know if I can control my dreams, but if I could, I would break up with him in a heartbeat. I can't believe he would hurt me like that. He was like a different person, filled with rage and dangerous passion.

And then there's Will. Poor Will. He doesn't want to be tangled up in all this. He was just in the wrong car at the wrong time. And I smiled. And Cole hated that smile. How could a simple smile morph my boyfriend into an abusive, unbridled monster? He knows I would never cheat on him. And Will would never hook up with someone who had a boyfriend. Would he?

Evelyn stopped writing to contemplate what Will would ever do if Dream Evelyn made a move on him. She could do that kind of thing in the 2000s. Would he be too shy to reciprocate, or would he surprise her and take control? She knew she wouldn't find out unless she broke up with Cole.

A loud bang stunned her, and Evelyn dropped her pen. Two more bangs. "Evelyn?"

In the throes of panic, it took her a moment to register that Mr. Allen was back from lunch and knocking on the locked door. Her heart was beating so fast she could hardly catch her breath, and her knees were weak as she walked to the door to unlock it. She'd been so lost in her thoughts and her writing that the entire lunch hour had flown by. She tried to take a deep breath and compose herself before letting her boss in, but the banging on the door brought back the memory of the gunman in the alley—and the gunman at the party in her dreams, if she was honest—and had left her paranoid and pale. Mr. Allen noticed something was wrong the moment she opened the door.

"Evelyn, are you all right?" he asked, confused. "You look like you've seen a ghost!"

"Yes, I'm sorry. I forgot I locked the door, and—" She inhaled sharply, trying not to cry in front of her boss.

"Evelyn, has something happened? Sit down. You're shaking." He gently guided her down to the sofa. His fatherly nature and caring aura were all Evelyn needed to break her completely in two. On the verge of sobbing, she put her head in her hands and leaned forward. Mr. Allen offered his handkerchief, unsure of what to do.

Once she had composed herself a bit, Evelyn sat up straight, embarrassed. "I'm sorry. This is so unprofessional."

"Nonsense. What's wrong? Perhaps I can help?"

A few minutes later, Evelyn was sitting across from Mr. Allen. He reached into his bottom desk drawer and pulled out a bottle of brandy. Evelyn was slightly surprised. She didn't know Mr. Allen drank, but they'd never been in a drinking situation together. He poured the caramel-colored liquid into two snifters, sliding one across the desk toward her. She reached for the glass, hesitantly taking a sip. The alcohol was strong on her lips and tongue and warmed her throat immediately. Blinking a few times to get used to the bitter taste, Evelyn took another sip. She quickly decided the beverage was not for her and placed the glass on the edge of the desk. She stared at her boss, unsure of where to begin.

"Now, if you're comfortable, please tell me what has you so upset," he implored.

Once Evelyn started talking, she couldn't stop. She told Mr. Allen about the man in the alley the other day and about his gun against her head. She described how paranoid and jumpy she'd been since it happened. She even told him she'd had dreams about being held at gunpoint. She didn't elaborate on the dreams because they were a lot to unpack, but by the time she was finished, Mr. Allen was sitting back in his chair, astonished.

"Evelyn, I had no idea. I am so sorry." He put his hand over his mouth. "It's my fault. I should have never let you take that alley! If I had known you were going home that way, I would—"

"No! It's not your fault at all! I just think I might need more time—and maybe some help—to get rid of the paranoia, you know?"

He wrote something down on a scrap of paper. Sliding it across the desk to her, he said, "My nephew. He's a therapist."

Evelyn's eyes widened at the suggestion.

"Well, he's going to be a therapist." Mr. Allen corrected himself. "He's almost done with his doctorate at the university. He's specializing in how to move on from trauma. He's been working with some soldiers from the war to recover from some of the horrors they saw on the front lines. I'm sure he might have some words of wisdom for you as well."

Holding the paper in her hand, Evelyn bit her lip. "Thank you." She didn't know what else to say. She was worried if people knew she was going to visit a therapist, they would think she was crazy.

"You're most welcome. If you'd like, I can have him meet you here at the office."

"No, that won't be necessary." She folded the slip of paper and held it in her hand. "You are so kind. I'll pay him a visit soon, I promise." She sat up in her seat and straightened her skirt. "I guess I should get back to work!"

"Why not take the afternoon off to gather your thoughts and rest?" Mr. Allen suggested. "I don't have much for you to do this afternoon anyhow."

Evelyn almost cried again at her boss's kindness. She gratefully accepted his offer and gathered her things.

He accompanied her down the hallway, onto the elevator, and through the lobby. Once on the sidewalk, he raised his arm to signal a cab. After making sure Evelyn was safely in the back seat, Mr. Allen handed the driver some money from his coat pocket. "You get home safely and let me know if there's anything I can do."

"I don't know how to thank you." She barely got it out before the driver tipped his hat and Mr. Allen shut the door, raising his hand to wave at Evelyn through the window as the cab pulled away. Evelyn retrieved the scrap of paper Mr. Allen had given her earlier.

Thomas Allen.

She didn't know why she was surprised his last name was Allen. He was her boss's nephew, after all. Wondering if she should take Mr. Allen up on his advice and pay Thomas a visit, she stared at the address her boss had scribbled down. Part of her almost asked the driver to make a detour so she could go and talk to Thomas immediately, but she reconsidered. It wasn't the done thing for a woman in 1919 to see a therapist, and she wasn't sure she could do it without anyone finding out.

Folding the piece of paper up and putting it back into her pocket, Evelyn relaxed in the cab, trying to lose herself in the sights of the city as she headed home.

Chapter 14
1919

A couple of days had passed since Evelyn had broken down at work in front of Mr. Allen, and a couple of nights since she dreamed about Cole abusing her after she'd come home from the rally with Will.

After work, Evelyn took a cab to the address Mr. Allen had given her. The stigma around seeing a therapist had caused her so much stress she'd barely been able to eat. Still, she had mostly convinced herself it was all right because Thomas wasn't a real therapist until he finished school. It would really just be two young people talking, she rationalized. She needed help, and she couldn't simply go on with life hoping she'd never have another embarrassing breakdown. Evelyn spent the ride second-guessing whether she should go through with the meeting or if she should ask the driver to drop her off at home. Before she could decide, the car pulled up outside a row of brownstones. She glanced at the piece of paper in her hand and up at the building numbers to get her bearings. In a few moments, she was knocking on the door of a house with two regal lion statues flanking the gate out front. A friendly faced older woman answered.

"Good evening, I'm Evelyn Moore. My boss, Mr. Gerald Allen, gave me this address for a Mr. Thomas Allen, his nephew?"

The woman smiled, opening the door wider and beckoning Evelyn inside. "Ah, yes. Gerald told me you might be coming by to talk to Thomas! I'm Nancy Allen, Thomas's mother and Gerald's sister-in-law."

"I've heard so many wonderful things about your family, Mrs. Allen. Your brother-in-law speaks very highly of you and Thomas."

"Well, that's a relief." The older woman grinned back at Evelyn.

She followed Mrs. Allen down a long hallway and eventually into a small but well-appointed library. Evelyn blushed when their entrance interrupted a young man seated in an armchair in the corner of the room, his head down, lost in a book. He quickly stood up, placing the book on a small side table.

As he turned to face them, Evelyn took him in. He wasn't conventionally handsome, but he was unassuming and had a gentle face.

"Ms. Evelyn Moore, this is my son, Thomas." Nancy gestured proudly toward him. "Thomas, Ms. Moore is your uncle Gerald's secretary at the law office."

Thomas's eyes lit up when he recognized who Evelyn was. "Ms. Moore!" He pulled another armchair closer to the one he'd been sitting in. "Pleased to meet you. My uncle mentioned you might stop by."

"Thank you for taking the time to talk to me." Evelyn was suddenly shy. "I know this is peculiar."

"Not at all." He smiled warmly. "I'm happy to take my studies out for a test drive, if you're willing to trust me." He motioned for her to sit in the chair he'd pulled over. "Mother, if you wouldn't mind, I think Ms. Moore and I have some things to discuss."

"Oh, of course." Nancy turned to leave. "I'll just be reading in the other room." To her son's embarrassment, Mrs. Allen flashed a hopeful look at the pair before she closed the doors and left them.

Alone in the small, dimly lit library, Evelyn and Thomas faced each other, neither one knowing exactly how to start.

"I hope you're not nervous." He sat. "It can be a little strange, talking to a stranger about such private things."

"I suppose." Evelyn shrugged. "I'm just so desperate to feel safe again that I'll try anything."

"My uncle told me what happened to you in the alley after work."

She was relieved she didn't have to recite the entire story.

"I imagine you've been having a hard time feeling safe anywhere after that."

"I don't know how to be alone anymore." She cast her gaze on the crackling fire. "A few days ago, I was fine walking home alone or being in the office by myself for an hour. Now, I'm afraid there's someone with a gun waiting to pounce on me around every corner."

"That's not unusual after a traumatic experience. It's only been a few days, hasn't it?"

"It's been a few days since the first attack—" Evelyn realized she'd misspoken and lumped the alley attack and the gunman at the party in her dreams together as she'd started speaking to Thomas. "I mean, since the alley, and—"

"Did this happen more than once?" His brow furrowed in concern.

"No!" she said quickly. "Well, yes. I mean, it happened again in my dream. I got held at gunpoint in a dream. After the alley. Sorry, I didn't mean to confuse you."

Thomas perked up. "Tell me more about the dream."

"Well, no, the dream isn't the problem." She shook her head. "I'm sure I just dreamed about it because of what happened in the alley. I dream a lot. It's nothing." She paused in her rambling, flustered.

"Actually, dreams are something I'm focusing on in my studies," he said, sitting forward in his seat. "I think they're fascinating. Dreams can help explain the psyche, almost like a temperature check for the mind. Some of the soldiers I've worked with have dreams that actually tell me a lot about how best to treat them." He paused. "Perhaps your dreams could help us figure out how to heal you from your attack." Evelyn's face changed, and Thomas hoped he hadn't upset her.

"I suppose that would be all right. If you like dreams, you'll probably love my ongoing saga!" she quipped.

"Ongoing?" He raised his eyebrows. "What do you mean?"

She hesitated as she considered how to explain or if she even should. "Well, I just mean I can tell you the whole story of my dream life." She'd already come this far, so she might as well tell him. "I dream about it every night." Immediately, her face turned red. She barely knew this poor man and wondered if she'd taken his credentials too seriously. Maybe she was getting too comfortable with him too quickly. When she glanced up at him, he was eagerly leaning in to hear more.

"So, you're saying you go to sleep, dream about something, wake up, and then when you go back to sleep, the dream picks up where you left off?" he asked.

"Well, yes, I suppose so. It's as if I'm watching a film of my life, only it's not my life, exactly. It's more like—" She was having trouble explaining herself. "It's like I have two lives, but one of them is a dream." She wasn't ready to tell him the dream life happened almost a century in the future.

His eyes lit up even more now. He stood and hurried to the desk for a notepad and a pencil. Sitting back down, he scribbled something. "How long has this been happening?"

"My whole life, I suppose. I can't remember a time when I didn't have the dreams."

"And you remember all of them? The dreams?"

"Most of them. I mean, I record them so I won't forget. It can get hard to keep it all straight."

"Okay, listen. I know you're here tonight because you need help with the alley attack, and we're absolutely going to do that for you," he said. "But I gotta tell you, this dream thing, this could really be something interesting."

Evelyn was confused. She hadn't come here to talk about her dreams, and she wasn't even sure how they'd gotten so off-topic. "I don't understand. They're just dreams, just my brain making things up, aren't they?"

"Ms. Moore, no one I've ever heard of dreams consecutively like you do. Most of us, myself included, have one-off dreams that make little to no sense, and when we wake up, they end. We start over the next night, blank slate. No continuation. Have you ever done that?"

She thought back. "No," she admitted. "It's always just picked up where it left off. I thought it was how some people dream! My own parents never believed me when I told them about it." She wasn't sure why she'd become so defensive of her dreams suddenly. No one had ever really asked about them before. She hadn't openly shared that part of her life with anyone since she was a child, and Thomas asking to study her dreams set off alarm bells inside her head.

Sensing her uneasiness, Thomas placed the notepad on the side table with the book he'd been reading when Evelyn first entered. "Let's put the dreams aside for now. Tell me more about the alley."

She relaxed and took a deep breath before settling back into the chair and telling Thomas about the man in the alley. As she spoke, telling him the same story she'd told her boss earlier that week, Evelyn's mouth became parched and her heart rate sped up again. She paused to catch her breath.

He stood and headed toward a sideboard table. "If you get overwhelmed, we can stop at any time." He poured her some water. "Just say the word."

She smiled and took the glass from him. His presence was warm and safe, and she was already calming down again as if she'd known him for years.

An hour later, Evelyn had taken Thomas through the details of the attack in the alley. She told him how she'd broken down in her office on Monday at the very thought of being alone, and a knock on the door had sent her spiraling into a full-blown panic attack in front of his uncle. He listened so well she kept forgetting she was with a man she barely knew.

He offered her a few suggestions on how to center herself when the fear started rising and talked her through what he called coping mechanisms. They practiced some breathing exercises to help get her body out of panic mode, and he explained the science behind it. He was fascinating to talk to, and his advice came so genuinely that she couldn't help but trust him.

Soon, Mrs. Allen walked into the room, interrupting the conversation. "I just wanted to check on you two and make sure you didn't need anything." A smile curled the sides of her mouth.

"We're fine. Thank you, Mother," Thomas said.

"Actually, I should go." Evelyn realized she'd probably overstayed her welcome. She stood to gather herself, embarrassed that she'd spoken so freely and for so long to this man she had known merely a couple of hours.

"I'll let you say your goodbyes," Mrs. Allen said. "It was lovely to meet you, Ms. Moore."

"You as well. Thank you, Mrs. Allen." She meant it. She had taken an immediate liking to Nancy. "I look forward to seeing you again."

Nancy turned and left the room, leaving the door to the library open.

Evelyn turned to Thomas. "Thank you for taking the time to talk to me. I know you probably had other plans for this evening. I didn't mean to occupy your whole night."

He stood and walked with her toward the door. "Not at all. In fact, it's been a while since I've had the pleasure of such a scintillating conversation with anyone on or off campus, so thank you."

Amused by his wit, she stopped before they went through the library door and turned to face him. "Oh, I'm sure you speak to people much more interesting than me."

"You'd be surprised how boring most academics are." More seriously, he added, "I've thoroughly enjoyed your visit. I hope you'll come again."

"Of course. I'd like to continue our chat sometime!" She genuinely did want to see him again.

"And of course if you don't mind, I would love to dig a little more into those dreams you were talking about."

She swallowed. "I don't usually talk to people much about that, but I'll think about it," she promised.

Upon leaving Thomas's house, Evelyn was strangely light on her feet. She was happier than she had been when she arrived. She chalked it up to having just released some of her innermost fears and taken some steps to overcome them. She took a cab most of the way home but walked the last two blocks to practice the breathing exercises Thomas had taught her. Evelyn silently thanked him for his help and resolved to meet with him again soon.

Chapter 15
2003

Evelyn woke up more confident after meeting Thomas in her dream. Some of the things he'd taught her about how the body responds to frightening things had already given her more control of her emotions in her other life, and—she hoped—left her more prepared to react in a dangerous situation in both her lives.

Her morning classes had been canceled due to a burst pipe in the political science building, so her new plans included scouring her apartment for anything and everything that belonged to Cole and piling it up so she could get every reminder of him out of her home and her life. She didn't want to be around him after what had happened the other night. Every time she saw that pillow, her mind sent her right back to the moment when Cole had thrown it across the room at her right before he had attacked her. They hadn't spoken since.

She'd always promised herself she would have a zero-tolerance policy for violence when it came to the men she dated, and after what Cole had done, she knew this was the time she had to make good on that promise. In spite of her resolve, she kept questioning herself, wondering if it really counted since he hadn't actually hit her.

Angry with herself for making excuses for him, she slammed her fist down on the kitchen counter. She couldn't give him another chance, but there was a small part of her that also couldn't discount that he'd saved her life at the party. Her mind struggled to reconcile the man who had assaulted her with the man who had stood in front of a gun for her.

Evelyn got out an old moving box and began filling it with Cole's belongings. He'd spent so many nights with her that he'd left clothes, hats, schoolbooks, CDs, and even a stick of deodorant at her apartment. She began folding the clothes before she realized he didn't deserve it and instead tossed them haphazardly into the box.

As she packed up Cole's things, her mind wandered back to her dream the night before. She couldn't help but smile every time she thought about Thomas. His personality had ignited something in her, and she wanted to spend more time talking to him. He took her by surprise because he wasn't anything like the men she was typically attracted to. He certainly wasn't anything like Calvin. Or Cole, thank goodness.

Evelyn hoped she'd see Thomas again soon. Replaying their conversation in her mind, she fixated on the part where he'd said her dreams were unusual and that he might know more about them. She'd never really thought the dreams were that different, but when she'd brought them up to her parents around age seven, they'd reacted so strangely she became fearful of ever speaking of it again. They'd looked at each other in such a way that Evelyn knew this topic was something they did not want to discuss. They sat her at the kitchen table and spent an hour trying to convince Evelyn she was mistaken, instructing her not to tell anyone else about the dreams. They hadn't specified why, exactly, and Evelyn hadn't asked. She complied with their requests, lied, and admitted she'd made up the dreams to end the conversation, and then simply didn't talk about her dreams anymore. If her own parents couldn't accept her dreams, she was sure no one would. So she'd kept them a secret ever since. Even from Cammie.

In her dream life, when she'd approached her parents, they had angrily forbidden her to speak of her dreams to anyone again and harshly warned her someone may think she was insane and have her carted off to an asylum. She had been shocked at their response as they were typically kind and gentle people. After that, she'd been too self-conscious and afraid of being whisked away from home by someone in a white lab coat to bring up her dreams to anyone in that life. Until Thomas.

She wondered if he might be able to tell her more about how rare it was to dream about another life and if it would ever stop. She'd always thought there must be more people out there who dreamed the same way but had never stopped to think about it being such a rare phenomenon. She wasn't sure how he'd react to finding out her dreams took place several decades in the future.

Suddenly, Evelyn stood up straight, a pair of Cole's basketball shorts halfway into the box.

It's 2003, she thought. *What if someone else has studied dreams like mine since 1919?*

Evelyn stuffed the remainder of Cole's belongings in the box and hurried to her laptop. She didn't really know what to search for but fidgeted with her hands, excited at the prospect that there may be more people like her in the world. She took a deep breath as she typed into the search bar, "dreaming consecutive dreams." It was as good a start as any. Evelyn scanned the results, desperate for anything that sounded like what she had experienced her whole life. After the third page, she was ready to give up when she noticed a search result from a small science web magazine. The article was titled, "Are Your Dreams Actually Time Travel?"

Evelyn's heart pounded as she clicked the link and waited for the page to load. She'd never even considered her dreams might be time travel. Was that even possible? She hadn't thought so. She scrolled through the article, becoming more and more intrigued. There were some quotes from an author who was a researcher specializing in the psychology of dreams. He had a theory that dreams could be what he called a "time travel mechanism," and that some people may have the ability to live in multiple timelines simultaneously.

Her head was swimming. *Timelines? That doesn't make any sense. You can't be in two places at once.* The article continued to describe several studies that supported his theory. Evelyn printed the article to save it, leaving it on her desk before hopping into the shower to get ready for her afternoon classes.

Chapter 16
2003

When their classes were over for the day, Evelyn and Cammie met for a quick dinner to catch up. Evelyn was desperate to get the choking incident with Cole off her chest even though she was sure Cammie would go ballistic when she found out what he'd done. Evelyn wanted Cole out of her life, but when he'd attacked her, she'd seen a side of him she wasn't sure how to navigate safely. She needed her best friend's support and signature fiery pep talk.

As they sat outside at a café near her apartment, Evelyn made small talk, building up the courage to tell Cammie what transpired with Cole the night before.

Before long, Cammie interrupted her. "Okay, Ev. What's wrong?" She knew Evelyn too well to buy her act.

Evelyn took a deep breath before explaining what had happened after the rally. Cammie listened without responding, but her face became red with anger, and her rage grew as her friend spoke. Cammie somehow managed to refrain from interrupting until Evelyn was done telling her story, but the second it was finished, she sprang into action.

"I'm gonna lose it," she growled, balling up her fists. She took a breath to compose herself before she continued. "Please tell me you broke up with him."

"Well, not yet. I mean, I haven't seen him or talked to him since it happened. I don't want to see him."

"You have to end it, Ev. You know you can't keep dating this man, right? This is how it starts. What if he kills you?"

Evelyn looked down at her plate. She didn't think Cole would go that far, but after he'd choked her, she realized she didn't really know him at all. She nodded and pursed her lips. "I'm just scared. I don't want him to get mad when I break up with him, you know?"

"That's why you have to do it in a public place! That way, he can't do anything nuts. Too many people around."

"Good idea." Evelyn nodded. "I'll tell him I want to go to dinner."

"No!" Cammie said loudly. "Not at night. It's safer in the daytime. Go to lunch. Or coffee. I can even come with you if you want! I can sit across the restaurant and keep an eye out."

Evelyn nodded, glad she'd told Cammie about Cole. "Do you think he'll leave me alone afterward?"

"I don't know." Cammie moved her chair closer and grabbed Evelyn's hand in support. "But I'm here, whatever you need. Okay?"

"Thanks." Evelyn hugged her best friend. Cammie was the sister Evelyn never had, and she was grateful they'd come to the city together.

After dinner, Cammie walked Evelyn to the front of her building before catching a cab home. Inside, Evelyn walked down the hall toward her apartment, fumbling in her purse for her keys with her head down. As she turned the corner near her front door, she almost bumped directly into someone. She lifted her eyes to apologize and inhaled sharply when she saw who it was. *Cole.* Her adrenaline began to rush at the mere sight of him. She tried not to panic.

"What are you doing here?" Her heart thumped with trepidation as she walked around him toward her apartment door.

"I want to talk," he answered, trailing her.

"There's nothing to talk about." She turned to face him, trying to appear confident and in control of her emotions. "I'll get your stuff. Wait here." She watched him out of the corner of her eye as she unlocked the door and opened it just enough to get herself inside. She closed the door in his face and locked it, leaving him in the hallway while she retrieved the box from the kitchen counter. When she opened the door, he was seething.

"So you're seriously just gonna break up with me now? Because we had one stupid fight?" His voice rose.

"One fight?" she whispered, trying not to yell in the hallway of her building. "You attacked me, Cole!"

"Oh my God!" Cole turned in disbelief, throwing his arms up in the air. "Are you serious right now? I didn't hit you! I didn't even hurt you!" He lowered his voice, moving closer to her. "You know I would never hit you, Evelyn. This is ridiculous."

She was trembling as she gripped the box, but she couldn't back down. Cammie's words echoed in Evelyn's mind. *What if he kills you?* She couldn't be in a relationship with someone capable of hurting her in any way. He'd shaken her to her core, and she wasn't going to end up dead at his hands. He wasn't worth it. She braced herself for his reaction to her impending rejection.

Her voice was slightly unsteady, but she asserted herself. "No, Cole, I *don't* know you'd never hurt me. Not after the other night. All I know is that you have a temper you can't control, and you have a major jealousy issue." She grew more confident as she spoke. "You need help. We are broken up. Please don't contact me anymore!" Shoving the box into his chest, she turned on her heel and walked back into her apartment. She slammed the door and locked it behind her again.

She immediately clapped her hand to her mouth, willing herself not to breathe too loudly. Even after her own brave performance, she was still scared of what he might do. When no noise came from the other side of the door, she slowly rose to look through the peephole. She fully expected him to be standing there ready to fight, but no one was in view. Slinking into her bedroom, she locked that door as well and sat down on her bed.

Her head in her hands, she tried to catch her breath. All her bottled-up feelings were bursting to come out. She climbed under the covers and pulled them up to her chin. Wrapping herself in the comforter, she closed her eyes and tried to think about Calvin. Thomas. Time travel. Anything but Cole.

Her thoughts drifted to Thomas, mainly. Which also brought her to Will. Between her dreams and her reality, she was in a pretty complicated inner love conflict that none of the men involved even knew about. But since she'd just broken up with Cole, one bachelor had been eliminated, and that certainly simplified things. She wondered if, now that she was single, she might work up the guts to talk to Will about her secret attraction to him. Her eyelids becoming heavy with the weight of the day, Evelyn almost drifted off.

Moments later, her doorbell rang, alarming her. Her heart pounding, she threw on a robe and walked to the door as the frantic ringing continued. She knew exactly who it was.

"What do you want, Cole?"

"Let me in. I left something there!" he yelled back angrily.

She paused. Should she open the door and let this nightmare continue? Or would he come in, get whatever he needed, and leave? Something told her to open the door. She grabbed a sharp knife from the block in the kitchen and clutched it as she turned the door handle. A sliver of hope said Cole could be mature, even for a moment. Opening the door only a crack and leaving the chain lock in place, she peered out into the hallway at him, saying nothing.

"I left my extra phone charger in there. I need it." She held the knife behind her back and hoped for the best as she removed the chain lock and let him in. He barged past her and into the bedroom. Closing the apartment door, she moved to the kitchen, not wanting to be in the same room as Cole. She heard him rustling around on her desk, unplugging the base charger for his phone and collecting the cord. Soon, he returned holding a charger in one hand and some papers in the other. She recognized them instantly as the research she'd printed earlier about time travel.

"What is this garbage?" He waved the papers in her direction. "Time travel? What is going on with you? You're psycho." Anger boiled inside her as he carried the papers toward the patio. Before she realized what he was doing, he'd opened the door and tossed the research over the balcony, the sheets coming apart in the wind and floating down into the street.

"Why would you do that?" she screamed, darting toward the patio to watch the papers scattering around the sidewalk and road. "I can't believe you would stand there and call *me* a psycho while you're throwing my stuff off the balcony!"

He walked past her through the living room to the front door. "If this is more of your weird dream journal stuff, I don't wanna talk about it. I'm out!" He hurled the door open and turned to face her before going. "I knew you were a cheater."

"What?" she yelled, her temper rising. "I've never cheated on you. Ever!"

"Whatever. Go hang out with your boyfriend from the rally! Maybe you two can talk about time travel." He stopped to add one more thing. "Good luck getting his dorky ass to take a bullet for you!" He slammed the door behind him, leaving her standing alone in the living room in front of the open balcony door. The sounds of city traffic and her angry breathing were all she could hear. She was as mad as she had been when he'd left the first time, only this time she was surer than ever that she was done with him. Forever. Watching him throw her papers over the balcony in some kind of jealousy-fueled rage was all the confirmation she needed that this man was not the one for her. She hated that her friends and family had been right about him but hoped they would give her grace as she worked her way forward from the relationship.

She wondered what it was that made her so steadfast about breaking up with Cole tonight as she pulled the balcony door closed, muffling the noise from outside, and drew the blinds shut. She entered her bedroom. Cole had made quite a mess of her desk. She sat down and opened her laptop to find the article about the time travel research again. She really wanted to read it and ask Thomas about it in her dreams. In a few minutes, Evelyn had found the page, printed a fresh copy, and gone down a rabbit hole of research about time travel and the people who believed they had experienced it in their dreams. Most of them talked about sleep being a mode of time travel, like falling asleep and waking up in the future, but not an entire ongoing life. That wasn't the same thing she experienced, and she couldn't find anyone who dreamed the way she did, going back and forth between what were, to her, two separate lives.

A bit frustrated, Evelyn almost closed the laptop, but first she sent Cammie a quick IM telling her she'd broken up with Cole and asking if Cammie could come over and spend the night. Evelyn was nervous that Cole might come back to her apartment in some sort of drunken rage and didn't want to be alone if he did. A few minutes later, Cammie called and said she was on her way. Sitting on her bed, Evelyn wrote in her journal while she waited.

I did it. I broke up with Cole. And I meant it. I'm not going back.

I'm free. I've felt his invisible hand around my throat every second since he attacked me. Until tonight. I can breathe again.

I don't know what this freedom means for me, but I know I dodged a major bullet by breaking it off with Cole, and I hope it leads me to something better. I'm lucky. A lot of women don't get out of these situations unscathed, and I hope this is the end of Cole's reign of terror in my life.

Evelyn closed the journal when she heard a knock at her door. She glimpsed through the peephole to make sure it was Cammie before she unlocked the door. Cammie walked in, a bottle of prosecco in hand. She knew her best friend very well, and when Evelyn did drink, she drank the bubbly stuff. Tonight struck her as an appropriate time to at least put the option on the table.

The two climbed into Evelyn's bed and each sipped a glass while they watched television and chatted. It was just the distraction Evelyn needed. Soon, much more secure with her best friend nearby, she closed her eyes and allowed herself to drift, hopefully, to talk to Thomas about the dreams and go on more extravagant dates with Calvin.

Chapter 17

1919

Evelyn didn't have to wait long to see Thomas again. She sat at her desk, typing up a letter for Mr. Allen, when the office door clicked open. Mr. Allen didn't have any meetings on the calendar for the morning, and she couldn't imagine who it might be. Her face lit up when Thomas walked in. He wore a long coat and carried his hat in his hand. He approached her, a smile on his face, as she stood to greet him.

"Ms. Moore!"

"Evelyn, please," she corrected. Surely the things they'd discussed in their meeting were personal enough they could be on a first-name basis.

"Evelyn." He scanned the reception area awkwardly, not knowing what to say next. She noticed he was endearingly shy, so she took over the conversation.

"What brings you all the way to this part of town this morning?" She hung his hat and coat on the rack for him.

"You, actually."

Evelyn eyed him quizzically. "Me?" she asked, returning to her desk and straightening some papers. "You came all the way here to see me?"

Immediately blushing, Thomas stumbled as he attempted to explain himself. "Well, I mean—I . . . your dreams! I wanted to show you something." He went to the coat rack, speaking excitedly as he fished in his coat pocket and pulled out a book. "I couldn't stop thinking about what you said. About how you travel back and forth between two timelines when you sleep. I thought—"

"Well, I don't know if I would call it that." Evelyn interrupted him, not ready to label her unique dream patterns as time travel *just* yet.

"Well, whatever is happening to you, this might explain some of it," he said, presenting her with the bound book. Taking it, she read the title aloud.

"*Dormant Projection: the Theory of Dreams as They Relate to Time Travel.*" Evelyn raised her eyebrows at him, waiting for him to elaborate.

"So this doctor who wrote this, Fletcher," he said, taking the book back from her and flipping through the pages to find something. "He's obsessed with studying dreams. One of my undergrad professors talked about this book, and your story made me think of it." He turned the pages as he spoke. "Fletcher conducted sleep studies in the 1880s and had the subjects record their dreams in journals. He studied dozens of people. He paid them to participate, so they gladly came to make a few dollars for their families."

Evelyn leaned forward to get a better look at the book's pages.

He continued. "Most of the subjects had normal dreams. They started and stopped every night, and they were always different. Usually related to things that had happened in the dreamers' lives that day. Sometimes they didn't make sense, so they would interpret the meaning of the dream and come up with the same conclusion: just a manifestation of what happened in their waking lives."

Evelyn examined the pages of the book intently as Thomas spoke, taking in everything he was saying.

Just then, Mr. Allen's office door opened, and her boss appeared in the hallway. His face lit up when he saw his nephew, then changed to confusion. "Thomas, my boy, what are you doing here?" he asked, reaching out to shake Thomas's hand.

"I actually came to talk to Ms. Moore. I have a book she might like to borrow."

Evelyn closed the book and waved it at her boss. "I'll be sure to give it a read. Thank you." She tucked the book into her bag. The older Mr. Allen eyed the pair inquisitively, his eyes darting from one to the other. Sensing he had interrupted something, he feigned checking his wristwatch and made a show of realizing he was late for something.

"I had better get back to work. I have Mrs. Newbury coming in to discuss her husband's will." He patted Thomas on the shoulder before walking back into his office, closing the door behind him. Thomas and Evelyn tried not to laugh at his uncle's sudden awkwardness and terrible acting.

"Listen, if you're interested, give that book a skim and come by tomorrow night. We can talk about it more." Quickly realizing his forwardness, he paused. "If you want to, of course."

Evelyn smiled. "That sounds wonderful. I actually have some things I wanted to share with you about the dreams as well!"

At her words, he immediately relaxed his shoulders, relieved that he hadn't totally bungled asking her out again. "I'd better get going. I have a meeting in a bit. Tell my uncle I said goodbye?"

"Of course." Evelyn surprised herself when a small wave of sadness washed over her when he said he was leaving so soon. She wasn't sure if it was because she was so eager to learn more about her dreams or because she enjoyed spending time with him. He was interesting, passionate, polite, and sweet. She couldn't picture him ever behaving like Cole. And he wasn't flashy or smooth like Calvin. He reminded her a bit of someone else. Will.

Turning her attention from men to work, Evelyn forced herself to get back to typing the letter Mr. Allen had left for her.

At the end of the workday, Evelyn stood in the lobby of her office building waiting for Calvin to pick her up. He hadn't told her where they were going, but he had mentioned that she didn't need to change from her work clothes, so she'd checked her makeup and hair and powdered her nose in the bathroom before leaving the office.

Eventually, a black car pulled up, and Calvin emerged from the back seat. Opening the building door for her, he greeted her with a light peck on the cheek. "Good evening, Evelyn."

Her stomach fluttered, and she smiled as she took his arm. She'd forgotten just how gorgeous he was. He held the door open for her, and sliding into the back seat next to her, Calvin tapped on the divider, signaling for the driver to take off.

"So, where are you whisking me off to tonight?" Evelyn asked, dying to hear the answer. He'd set the bar high with their first date at the Woolworth Building, and she couldn't wait to find out what he had up his sleeve next.

"I want to introduce you to a friend. He just opened his own place in Greenwich Village, and I promised to pay him a visit."

Evelyn was excited to find out what kind of surprise another one of Calvin's fancy friends had helped set up for them.

When they eventually pulled up to their destination, she climbed out of the car and Calvin took her arm. He led her toward a door with a sign above it that read "Chuckles & Cheers." Confused, Evelyn entered the building with him.

Inside was dark and didn't smell much like a fancy restaurant. It smelled like booze and cigarettes. A woman behind a hostess stand greeted them when they walked in. "Welcome to Chuckles 'n Cheers," she muttered. This was obviously not her dream job. "Two?"

Calvin leaned in closer.

"Listen, I'm friends with Bobby. He knows I'm coming tonight. He set me up with a table," he said, not as politely as Evelyn would have liked.

"Name?"

"Nelson."

She checked her list. "Sorry, I don't see anything here.

Instantly, Calvin's face changed. "Go get Bobby," he snapped.

The hostess was visibly taken aback. She told the pair to wait while she went to speak to her boss. Evelyn crossed her arms and looked at the floor but stayed silent so she didn't make it worse. She was surprised Calvin was acting this way. He'd been a complete gentleman until now. It was giving her flashbacks to Jekyll and Hyde with Cole. Eventually, the hostess returned with a shorter man who had a dark complexion and a sharp nose. The two men shook hands, greeting each other.

"Cal, you made it!" His face was red and sweaty. "I'm sorry about the mix-up. I forgot to relay the message about your table to Myra here. Totally my fault." He laughed loudly as he gestured at the hostess, who was understandably unamused.

Calvin turned to introduce Evelyn. "Bobby Davis, this is my friend, Ms. Evelyn Moore."

Allowing Bobby to kiss her right hand, Evelyn found herself perturbed at being introduced as such. They weren't officially an item, but part of her had not been prepared for the sting of the word *friend*.

Bobby led the pair to a table in a smoky, dimly lit room where everyone faced a small stage. The blue curtain was drawn when they walked in, but Evelyn imagined this was where the "chuckles" part of the "Chuckles & Cheers" happened. Sitting down at a small table with Calvin, she couldn't help but be disappointed by going from the glamour of the Woolworth Building on their first date to this dark, seedy comedy bar. Still, she did enjoy comedy and held out hope that the night would surprise her. She smiled at Calvin as the lights darkened and the waitress brought their first round of drinks. Evelyn settled back in her chair, determined to make the best of the evening as the emcee strutted out in front of the curtain to start the show.

An hour and a half later, Evelyn and Calvin exited the comedy club, the brightness of the city streets harsh on their eyes after the darkness of the bar. Evelyn couldn't wait for the date to end.

Outside the bar, Calvin pointed out a small diner down the street. "Do you want to grab something to eat?"

Evelyn racked her brain for a way to get out of spending any more time with him. "Actually, those drinks at the show are getting to my head. I should probably go home and get some sleep," she lied. She hadn't even finished one drink.

His face changed from soft to stiff, and he squared his shoulders. "I see." His tone of voice sent chills up her spine. It reminded her of Cole.

"I had a wonderful time, though. I wish I could stay longer, but my head really is pounding." She hoped he was buying it. She had a familiar sense of needing to placate this man to avoid trouble. Reaching her hand up to gently touch his face, Evelyn smiled at him, trying desperately to appear smitten. "We'll go out again soon. I promise."

He relaxed a bit. "Tomorrow night." It was more an order than a question.

"Well, tomorrow night I can't. I—" She paused, not wanting to mention her plans with Thomas. Her dreams with Cole had taught her better, and her gut said to use the same strategy here. "It's my friend's birthday," she fibbed. "Maybe next week one night?"

"All right. I'll be in touch, Evelyn." He appeared to have calmed down a little. "Can I get you a car? I'm going to have a few more drinks with Bobby inside."

"Certainly, thank you." She was relieved she'd dodged what surely would have been a tense interaction with Calvin. Soon, she was in the back seat of a cab, headed for home. She pondered everything that had happened at the comedy club, becoming more and more disgusted as she replayed it in her mind.

He had been rude to the hostess, and she'd put that aside, assuming it was a one-off. But it hadn't been. Throughout their time at the bar, Calvin treated their waitress poorly. The way he spoke to her like she was a servant humiliated Evelyn. She didn't care how much money he had. That behavior was something she had been brought up to not tolerate. He laughed at some of the most off-color jokes she'd ever heard. The comedian at the club told racist, sexist, and altogether inappropriate jokes about the Great War. Mortified, she sat next to Calvin as he laughed uproariously at them all. She was shocked he found that type of humor funny and couldn't help but question what kind of a man he was. When she arrived at her apartment building, she was disappointed that the too-good-to-be-true man she'd met was officially just that.

Flopping onto her bed, Evelyn sighed out loud. She reached for her journal.

Today was a strange day.

I was really looking forward to my date with Calvin, but turns out he's less a dream and more a nightmare! He and I share none of the same values. I can't tolerate someone who thinks women are inferior to men or that anyone's skin color could make them superior to others, even if they are just laughing at a joke someone else told. I'm glad I found out sooner rather than later, but still, a disappointment.

Happily, however, Thomas paid me a visit at the office this morning, which was a welcome surprise. I wasn't expecting it, and I found myself giddy at the sight of him. I admit he has my interest, but I'm afraid my dreams might be more interesting to him than I am. I hope I'm wrong. He intrigues me more each day.

Thomas brought me a book about dreams and time travel. I suppose it's time to face the idea, as overwhelming as it is. Imagine, me, a time traveler! It sounds absolutely ridiculous when I think about it, but here I am, about to explore the possibility. I don't know what I'll do when I learn the answers, but I can't imagine having a chance at finding out and not jumping at it. I'm ready.

She closed the journal and got up to open her bag. She pulled out the book Thomas had given her and curled back up on her bed, settling into her pillows to begin reading.

Chapter 18
2003

Evelyn and Cammie sat at a high-top table surrounded by excitable bar-goers. The music was loud, and the atmosphere was fun, but Evelyn struggled to be present in the moment. Cammie had practically forced her to come out with her friends from her nursing classes, hoping to cheer her up with a good old-fashioned girl's night.

Evelyn scanned the bar, wondering which of the couples would make it through the month. The week, even. She was finding all the wrong men in all the wrong places lately. Cole had turned out to be an abusive monster, and Calvin was quickly revealing a side of himself Evelyn couldn't tolerate in her dreams or her real life.

"Ev, you there?" Cammie waved her hand in front of Evelyn's face.

Jolted out of her thoughts, Evelyn smiled at her friend and raised her drink. "I'm here, sorry! I'm just exhausted. It's been a long few days."

"Well, don't crash out on us yet." Cammie pointed toward the bar. "We've got shots coming!"

Evelyn sighed and shook her head, smiling. Cammie knew she hated taking shots but thought it was polite to order her one anyway. It was a running joke they had. Evelyn often ended up just sipping on them until they were gone, like a regular drink, but every now and then she surprised them—and herself—and knocked one back with no trouble.

Just then, a tray of shots appeared on the table. Cammie's friends Amanda and Casey handed out the shots and raised their glasses in a toast.

"To Evelyn dumping her horrible boyfriend!" yelled Casey. The girls cheered loudly, tapping their shot glasses on the table before downing the drinks. Evelyn drank almost all of hers, happy it tasted more like melon than anything.

Just then, someone patted her shoulder. Evelyn turned. Will was standing behind her, holding a bottled beer. A grin appeared on her face.

Enjoying a little liquid courage, Evelyn hugged him and introduced him to her friends. "Cammie, Casey, Amanda, this is Will. He's in my poli sci classes, and we run the anti-war group together."

Will greeted each of the girls with a friendly nod and a hello. Cammie made eyes at her, trying to figure out who her new friend was and if Evelyn liked him. Not wanting Cammie to say anything embarrassing, Evelyn turned to Will and gestured toward the bar. "Fresh drink?"

As they waited for their beverages, she racked her brain for something witty to say, but nothing clever came to her. Finally, Will handed Evelyn her cocktail and broke the silence.

"How are you doing after the whole party thing?"

Evelyn raised her eyebrows at the question. Cole hadn't checked on her once after the party. "I'm okay, actually." She'd never noticed how stunning his eyes were. They were a deep green with gold flecks that sparkled as he moved. "You have really pretty eyes," she blurted.

"Thanks." He dramatically batted his eyelashes. Evelyn laughed. He was a breath of fresh air after all the uptight, moody men she'd dealt with lately. He reminded her a bit of Thomas. They both had a way of making her feel at home.

"Seriously, how is your boyfriend healing up? Cole, right?" Will asked, snapping her back to reality. "Is his head any better?"

"*Ex*-boyfriend," she corrected. "And no, his head will never be better. He's a perpetual idiot." She took another sip of her drink, rolling her eyes.

Will stifled a laugh. "Ah, sorry. I wasn't aware you'd broken up. Didn't he just save your life or whatever last week? What happened?"

Evelyn scoffed at the idea of Cole being a hero. "Yeah, well, turns out that didn't mean he loved me enough not to put his hands on me a few days later."

"Wow, really?" He straightened up. "Are you serious? What did he do?"

Evelyn almost regretted bringing up Cole attacking her. She didn't want to put a damper on her night or Will's. "Can we talk about it some other time? I'm trying to forget it for tonight."

He leaned against the bar again, facing her. "I really am sorry you had to go through that. We don't have to talk about it anymore, but just so you know, I'm here if you do ever want to talk."

His kindness warmed her heart. She wasn't sure if it was her emotions or the drinks, but she made a mental note to order water next time the bartender came around. "Thanks, I appreciate that," she said. "So, what have you been up to this week?"

"Not much." He shrugged. "I got into a new show I've been watching, and I've mostly just been zoned in on that all week."

"What show?"

"It's this weird show about time travel and stuff, kinda dorky. I'm sure I'm probably the only person on earth who watches it. I love time travel stuff."

Evelyn perked up at that. She had the urge to tell him about her dreams and how she and Thomas thought maybe they were somehow a part of time travel. Opting not to completely freak him out, she kept her mouth shut and ordered water from the bartender instead.

"Hey, you wanna go outside? It's a little hot in here."

Will led her through the crowd and out to the patio, where about a dozen other patrons stood smoking cigarettes, drinking, and talking more loudly than they probably realized. The crispness of the outside air was refreshing after the stuffiness of the bar. Evelyn found them a small empty table with two chairs where they could sit and chat.

As they talked, Evelyn noticed they had a natural connection, and perhaps slightly fueled by alcohol, she took the leap and brought up her dreams. Of all the people she knew, perhaps he would understand or at least think it was interesting. She just hoped he wouldn't run for the hills.

"You know how you said you're watching a show about time travel?"

He nodded.

"Okay, so, promise you won't think I'm a freak if I tell you this?"

Will reached out his hand, his little finger sticking out. "Pinky swear I won't think you're a freak." He chuckled. They hooked their pinkies together briefly, sealing the deal.

"Okay, well, I have these dreams." She contemplated how to explain it. "I've been having them my whole life. But not like recurring dreams. They're not the same, ever."

He put his drink down and leaned in closer.

She continued. "It's like my dreams are a whole other life. The person in the dreams is me, but I've grown up with her. Alongside her? I don't know how to explain this."

"Wait, so you're saying your dreams are like a soap opera? Like every dream is a different episode, but it's the same story?"

"Yes!" Evelyn cried, amazed that someone had understood and explained her dreams in such a clever way. "Exactly. Except the soap opera is about me. And a bunch of people I don't know in real life." She laughed, knowing how odd it all sounded. He was silent long enough for Evelyn to convince herself she'd just officially lost any chance with him.

"Okay, that's the coolest thing I've ever heard!" Will was genuinely awestruck. "You gotta tell me more!" He rested his elbows on his knees and folded his hands under his chin. "Tell me what's happening in your dreams right now. Like, what happened last night?"

Though she was utterly relieved, Evelyn hesitated to get into so much detail about her dreams. Still, something about him made her just as comfortable as she'd been when she spoke with Thomas. She figured if he hadn't decided she was nuts so far, maybe he would be okay with all the rest.

"Okay. Um, let's see. So, in last night's dream I was at work. My dream job. Well, not the job of my dreams, but the place where I work in my dreams—" Evelyn paused, struggling to articulate her confusing set of circumstances.

"No, I got it." Will nodded.

Evelyn relaxed her shoulders, relieved he was following. "So I was at work, and my friend Thomas came by unexpectedly," she began. "He had a book he wanted me to read. It was actually about time travel." She glanced at his face to see if the phrase struck a chord. It did.

His eyes widened, and he smiled. "That's weird. We were just talking about that inside!"

"Yeah, that's not the only weird thing," she replied. "So this book, it basically says that sleep and dreams might be a mechanism for time travel. Like when I go to sleep, I might be slipping into a whole other timeline. Another plane, where I'm the same and the world is the same, but just in a different year." She stopped to take a breath, realizing she'd been talking really fast.

"Whoa, okay, so you're saying you think that's what your dreams might be?" He sipped his beer. "You think you might be falling asleep and traveling back in time to—when?"

"Right now, 1919. It's like, eighty years ago or something. Eighty-four, actually." She was growing self-conscious. She wasn't sure if his questions were him trying to understand, or if he had decided she was off her rocker.

"That's so awesome!" he exclaimed. "So you might get to live through prohibition and stuff and all the cool flapper parties and like, Gatsby and stuff?"

She giggled. She hadn't really thought of it that way. "I guess so, kinda?"

He considered that for a moment. His face turned serious. "Wait, did you just live through World War One in your dreams?"

"I did." Evelyn cast her eyes downward. "It was really, really tough. On *everyone*. It's one of the reasons I'm so against a new war now."

"That makes total sense," Will agreed. "I can't imagine."

Evelyn couldn't believe he was taking this all in so easily. "So you don't think I'm crazy?"

"First of all, I just pinky swore I wouldn't think that, so no." Evelyn chuckled as he continued. "No, I don't think you're crazy. This is the coolest, most honest thing I've heard in a really long time."

Her body relaxed as she realized he wasn't going to run for the exit, and the two chatted for another twenty-five minutes before Cammie came to inform Evelyn that Casey had reached her alcohol limit and needed to be taken home. Disappointed that she had to leave Will, Evelyn said her goodbyes, hugging him.

"Thanks for not thinking I'm a total weirdo!" she joked as she walked away.

"Takes one to know one!" He laughed, waving. Evelyn left the bar with Cammie and the girls, safe and happy for the first time in days.

When she arrived home, Evelyn went straight to her bedroom, chucking her bag and jacket on the bed as she jiggled the mouse on her laptop to make the screensaver disappear. She immediately checked her friend list to see if Will was online or not. His username was gray, indicating he wasn't active. She double clicked on his name to send him a message and stared at the blinking cursor, trying to decide what to write.

Finally, speaking out loud as she typed, she tapped out a message to Will. "Hey! Just wanted to say thanks again for not bailing on me as soon as I mentioned my weird dream thing. It means a lot." She almost hit send but paused, pursing her lips. She had just broken up with Cole and didn't want Will thinking she was using him as a rebound. She re-read the message and added one last thing.

"Let me know if you want to talk more about it sometime . . . it was good to have someone actually listen. Call/text me." She hit send before she could second guess herself but immediately regretted it. Surely Will would think she was coming on too strongly. She slammed the laptop shut to prevent any more damage that evening and, cursing herself for sending the message, went into the kitchen to make a snack. A few minutes later, waiting for the microwave to finish heating up her popcorn, Evelyn thought better of it and returned to the computer, opening it and typing a generic away message of her own in case Will came back and responded. He didn't, but Evelyn went to bed that night happy she'd somehow advanced her relationship with Will, whatever that meant. Hoping she'd wake to a message from him, she closed her eyes and let thoughts of her potential new love interest soothe her to sleep.

Chapter 19

1919

Good morning, journal!

I had the best dream about Will last night. He and I hit it off more than ever at the bar. But I'm worried about something.

I'm beginning to wonder if Thomas and Will are another set of parallels between my life and my dreams. Cole and Calvin are exiting my life at a similar time. Anyway, I'm not looking forward to breaking things off with Calvin, but it has to be done. Soon. I hope it's not anything like breaking up with Cole.

Evelyn checked the clock, scolding herself for running late. She shoved her journal into her bag and made her way to the office, hoping the day would go by quickly so she could head to Thomas's house and talk to him more about her dreams and the book he'd dropped off.

Throughout the day at work, Evelyn skimmed through the book, stopping every few pages to marvel at how much some of the dreamers' experiences mirrored hers. Some had dreamed of eras much closer to their own than hers, and some had dreamed of times hundreds of years apart. Some lived lives in two faraway places, and others, like hers, were in the same city but a different time. All the dreamers essentially lived two lives the same way she did, and apparently some handled it better than others. A few stuck out to her.

In 1883, Fletcher studied Albert Gershner, a railroad worker from Kentucky who dreamed of himself living another life during the Elizabethan Age in England. Albert had found Fletcher after traveling to New York for a sleep study in an attempt to figure out what his dreams meant. According to the doctor's notes from the studies, Albert had a hard time with the extreme differences in time, place, customs, and language, and keeping them all straight had messed with his head so much that he'd ended up being carted off to facilities for the mentally ill more than once during the time he'd worked with Fletcher.

Caroline Huber from somewhere outside of Toronto had come to the US to work as a nanny for a well-to-do family in New York when she was twenty years old in 1885, but every night she dreamed of a life upstate in the late 1960s, where she said men wore baggy, flowery shirts and had long hair, and music was the language of love. Caroline had ended up addicted to a cocktail of sleeping pills and opiates in her real life because she'd loved the 1960s so much, and she wanted to dream as much as possible so she could spend all her time there.

Others had fared better than Albert and Caroline, according to the book. One woman, Rosetta, spent her life going back and forth between being a laundress in Palermo and being a Vegas showgirl in the 1980s. She viewed her dreams as a gift and believed she'd been given an opportunity to predict the future. Because of this, her village in Italy revered her as a sort of oracle, and she lived a rather comfortable life in both her dreams and her reality.

Reading their stories, Evelyn became emotional at the realization that she wasn't alone in this world and that there were indeed other people who dreamed of a whole separate life in another time. It validated everything she'd ever thought about her dreams. They were real. She wasn't crazy. And her parents—both sets—had been wrong all this time. Thomas couldn't possibly know the gift he'd given her by allowing her to discover the other dreamers.

She considered the ways she related to each of the people in the book. Like Albert, she was confused and frustrated with bouncing between two lives where technology and daily tasks were so different. She'd spent her school years going from all learning done on a slate board with chalk to another life where computer labs and videos in classrooms existed. Maybe the things in her dreams of the future were real, but school—and life in general—in the 1980s and 1990s had been a lot easier with the convenience of computers, calculators, and other devices that Evelyn's peers and teachers in the early 1900s could only dream of.

Evelyn sympathized with Caroline, who had come to New York City at a young age just as Evelyn had, seeking a more exciting life. She wondered what had happened to Albert, Caroline, and all the other dreamers in the book and if they'd ever found any answers about their dreams.

Of all the dreamers in the book, Evelyn identified with Rosetta the most. Like Rosetta, Evelyn's dreams hadn't caused her any trouble so far, aside from hangover emotions when she woke up some days. She wondered if Albert and Caroline had experienced some trauma in one of their timelines that had made them so unstable.

Evelyn had to get to work, so she closed the book and turned back to the desk full of paperwork Mr. Allen had left for her, forcing herself to focus. She stuffed the book back into her bag, excited to get to Thomas's house later and talk to him about it.

With her eye on the clock all afternoon, Evelyn sporadically sneaked in a few minutes of reading Thomas's book before she packed up her desk for the day and prepared to walk to his house. It was a beautiful evening, and she was confident enough to make the journey alone, especially since it wasn't dark yet. If she kept to the main roads and used the techniques Thomas had taught her, she assumed would be fine. She still carried her umbrella every day just in case. Carefully tucking the book into her bag, Evelyn almost didn't notice Mr. Allen come out of his office.

He spied the book and recognized it as the one Thomas had dropped off the day before. He quickly connected the dots. "Ah, I see Thomas's novel has you quite hooked!" He smiled.

Slightly embarrassed at being caught, Evelyn blushed as she turned to face her boss. "It is very interesting," she said sheepishly.

"Headed straight home?" Mr. Allen's eyes glinted.

"Um, no. Not exactly. I have somewhere to be in a bit."

"Well, enjoy your evening." He grinned knowingly. "I'll lock up behind you."

"Good evening, Mr. Allen. See you in the morning!" She hurried down the hall before he could ask any more questions. She knew he'd caught on to her plans with Thomas, and she hoped he wouldn't think anything untoward was happening between them.

When she reached Thomas's front door, she paused before knocking to make sure her hair was straightened and her skirt wasn't too wrinkled.

Nancy answered the door, flashing Evelyn a warm grin. "Ms. Moore! What a lovely surprise! Thomas didn't tell me you were coming, though I'm sure he knew. He always forgets to tell me these things!" She ushered Evelyn inside as she talked. "How are you, dear?" Nancy asked, smiling over her shoulder as she walked down the hall toward the library door.

"I'm well, thank you! It's so nice to see you again." She was genuinely happy to be in the presence of Mrs. Allen, who reminded her a bit of her own mother. They were both welcoming and nurturing. She wondered if Mrs. Allen would think differently of her if she knew Evelyn was a dreamer.

Gently rapping on the library door, Nancy called out to her son. "Thomas, Ms. Moore is here to see you." She clicked the door open, and Thomas jumped out of his chair, coming out from behind his desk to greet them.

Straightening his hair, he met them at the doorway as they entered the dimly lit room. He smiled at Evelyn. "Good evening."

Evelyn noticed him blushing and wondered if it was the shadows in the dark room or if he was getting flushed in her company. She secretly hoped it was the latter.

"Good evening." She beamed at him.

"Evelyn, would you like to stay for supper?" Nancy interrupted.

Evelyn noted the hope in Mrs. Allen's voice and looked at Thomas to gauge his reaction before she answered. He raised his eyebrows playfully, goading her to agree.

"If it's all right with Thomas, I'd be happy to," she said politely, delighting the older woman.

"Of course it's all right with me."

His mother clasped her hands excitedly at his answer.

"I'll go and tell the kitchen." Nancy turned to leave the library. Before closing the door, she glanced back at the young pair. They giggled when the door clicked shut behind her.

"I'm sorry, my mother can be a little . . . pushy," he said. "When it comes to my love life, I'm afraid I haven't given her much to be excited about, so when she thinks she's reeled one in for me, she can come on a little strong. Not much of an actress."

"For what it's worth, your uncle won't be landing any leading roles, either."

Thomas motioned for Evelyn to join him in the two armchairs by the fire. She sat down as he poured her some water. Handing her a glass, he sat in the chair directly across from her.

Thomas got straight down to business. "So, have you had a chance to read any of that book I dropped off for you the other day?"

Evelyn retrieved it from her bag and held it up. "The people in this book are *just* like me! I mean, I haven't read it all yet, obviously, but Rosetta—"

He cut her off, unable to contain himself. "Rosetta!" he cried. "She reminds me of you! I knew you'd like her."

"I am so glad I met you." The words tumbled out of her mouth before she had time to think. She rushed to do damage control. "I mean, I just don't know if I ever would have found out there was anyone else like me on this earth if you hadn't shown me this book. Thank you for that. It's already helped more than you know."

"It's nothing," he said. "You are—this is—the most interesting thing I've studied in a long time, even in school!"

Her heart sank a little at hearing he was primarily excited about her as far as she could advance his scientific knowledge. Evelyn forced a smile and took a sip of her water to avoid showing her disappointment. She stared at the fire, not knowing how to reply.

"And of course, getting to spend time with you is the real bonus." It was as if he'd been reading her mind.

Her face flushed, and Evelyn hoped he would think it was just the warmth of the fire. "Likewise." She smiled.

"So, I found out something interesting today while I was researching your dreams at the university library," Thomas said, his tone changing back to business-like.

"Oh?" Evelyn turned her gaze from the flames and fixed it on him.

"Well, the doctor who wrote that book you're reading, Dr. Fletcher, he had a partner. He's barely mentioned in the book, but look at the footnotes. His name is all over the research."

Evelyn took the book, flipping it open to a page with footnotes to find the partner's name. "Fletcher and Holstead?"

"Holstead was his partner." Thomas said. "He didn't write any books about their research. I don't know why he wasn't a part of this one Fletcher wrote."

"So what does this mean?"

"Well, I asked some of my research professors on campus if they knew anything about Fletcher, because it says in the back of the book he briefly taught in the philosophy department," Thomas said excitedly. "So anyway, after asking around, I found out this Fletcher guy died a few years back."

Evelyn squinted at him, confused about how someone being dead could be good news.

"But Holstead lives here, *in the city*! We could go talk to him. Find out what else he knows about the dreamers and ask why he stayed out of the book!"

Evelyn sat up straight, inhaling sharply. "I don't know, Thomas. Should we be going around knocking on strangers' doors asking them about my dreams? What if they think I'm crazy?"

"Evelyn, the man who studied people who time travel in their dreams for a living shouldn't be thrown by talking to another one now."

"True," she admitted. "But I don't want word getting out. I have a job. And I would like to keep my friends and get married someday. I don't want rumors flying about the odd girl from Manhattan who thinks she's a time traveler."

He leaned forward, taking her drink from her hand and placing it on the table next to his chair. He took both her hands in his. "No one is going to think you're strange. I promise."

She swallowed, her pulse quickening as his warm hands held hers. "All right." It was all she could say at the moment.

He let go of her hands, leaning back in his chair and handing her back her glass. "So, when should we pay old Holstead a visit?"

"Tomorrow?" she answered quickly, surprising herself at how eager she was to get more answers about the dreamers.

"Tomorrow it is." He slapped his hands on his knees to emphasize the finality of the plan. "You know, if we keep seeing each other every day like this, my mother will start planning our wedding," he joked, prompting a laugh from Evelyn.

They sat staring at each other, smiling. Neither had words, and although it was awkward, it was laced with flirtation and a mutual understanding, so the silence was in itself a clear sign of their attraction to each other.

Just then, Nancy walked in. "Dinner is ready! Shall we make our way to the dining room?"

Evelyn and Thomas snapped up in their seats, jolted out of the unspoken connection they'd just shared. He offered his arm, but to Nancy's delight, Evelyn gestured toward his mother, prompting Thomas to offer his arm to her, instead.

"Ah, Thomas. A girl after my own heart!"

"Mother, please," Thomas said quietly as the three headed toward the dining room. Evelyn walked behind them, happy to be in the warmth of such a loving home.

Chapter 20
2003

Evelyn's very first thought when she turned off her phone alarm and opened her eyes was Will. She hoped she hadn't said anything embarrassing at the bar the night before. Racking her brain trying to remember everything they'd talked about, she rolled out of bed and chugged half a bottle of water from her nightstand before opening her laptop.

She glanced at the time in the bottom right corner of her screen, squinting through her sleepy haze. It was already almost eleven o'clock. Annoyed with herself for sleeping so late, she checked her IMs for any new messages. Her heart skipped a beat. Will had sent her a message. She sat down to read it, whispering aloud to herself as she did.

"Hey! Had a great time with you tonight!" It was timestamped 3:26 a.m. She smiled, flattered that he'd been thinking of her at that ungodly hour. She considered her next move. It had only been a few days since she'd broken up with Cole, and starting something new so soon was probably a bad idea, but she was drawn to Will. She always had been. Debating with herself over whether to ask Will out or to let him take the lead, Evelyn concluded Will would never ask her out so soon after she'd broken up with a serious boyfriend, so if she wanted this to happen, she was going to have to do it herself. She took a deep breath and began typing.

"Hi! I had fun, too! Would you maybe want to get together again and continue our conversation?" She closed her eyes and hit the send button.

His away message popped up in response, and Evelyn figured he was still asleep. She went to the kitchen to find something to eat. Back at her desk a few moments later with a granola bar and a glass of orange juice, Evelyn noticed Will had written her back already. Excited, she read his reply aloud.

"Do you have plans tonight?"

She formulated a response. "Not yet," she wrote. Within seconds, he'd responded.

"I'll pick you up at 7?"

Giggling with excitement, Evelyn was surprised at how effortless things had been with Will so far. She had been worried that he'd be turned off when she asked him out instead of waiting for him to do it, but it hadn't bothered him at all. She was glad she'd asked him. She considered calling Cammie to ask what to wear but decided to keep it casual and pick her own outfit this time. It had been a while since she'd been this smitten with anyone. She wanted to keep it to herself a little longer.

A few hours later, Evelyn met Will outside. He walked around the car to open her door for her and greeted her with a warm embrace. The scent of his cologne sent tingles up her spine every time she smelled it.

As they pulled away from the building, Evelyn was happier than she had been in a long time. Trying to remember the last time she'd had real first-date butterflies like this, she realized she'd never had them with Cole. She briefly wondered if that had been a sign she should have paid more attention to but quickly resolved not to compare Will to Cole all night. There was no comparison anyway. Cole was clearly a monster, and Will was—so far—an absolute gentleman.

"Hungry?" Will asked, pulling up to a stop light.

"Starving!"

"I thought we'd go to that new place, Hearth. Is that okay?"

"Yes! Everyone's been talking about it! I've been dying to try it."

"I heard their ribeye is really good." He accelerated as the light turned green.

"Someone told me the pasta was the best they've ever had. But I do love ribeye. We might have to get both and share."

"Deal," he agreed, laughing.

"Thanks for coming out with me tonight."

"Thanks for asking me." He smirked. "I have to admit I wasn't expecting that."

"I hope you don't think it's too soon after I broke up with Cole. I don't want you to think I'm using you as a rebound or anything like that."

"It's not for me to say what you're ready for. Only you can know that," he reassured her. "It's just dinner, okay?"

"Okay." She smiled and relaxed in her seat, relieved that he was so understanding of her situation.

The pair soon arrived at the new restaurant that had opened only three weeks ago. The place was small and busy but not crowded. Evelyn was impressed with the well-appointed space. Will told the hostess he had a reservation, and she led them to their seats at a large slate bar at the far end of the room. Evelyn couldn't help but notice he'd gone to the trouble of calling ahead and making an actual reservation.

He pulled her chair out for her before he sat.

"Last night was fun. I'm glad I ran into you before I left the bar. I was on my way out when I saw you."

She was flattered that she was the only reason he stayed so late. "I had a really good time with you, too."

"I'd been meaning to check in and ask how you were doing after the party. I just figured you were busy taking care of Cole."

Evelyn put her hand gently over her heart, touched by this thoughtfulness. "I'm okay, really. There's been a lot going on lately, but I'm managing."

He sensed she didn't want to discuss Cole any further. "Let's change the subject. Tell me more about Evelyn."

"Like what?" She was curious what questions he might have for her.

"Well, so far I know you don't like coffee. I know about your dreams and that you're a politics junkie and an activist. Tell me something interesting about yourself I don't know yet."

Evelyn paused. She'd never really thought about herself as interesting. Outside of her dreams, nothing came to her off the top of her head. "I don't know. I guess I'm just a normal girl. Nothing special, really."

Will slapped his hand down on the bar, feigning shock. "Normal!?" he exclaimed. "Evelyn Moore, you are not normal."

She cocked her head, wondering what he'd say next.

"You're extraordinary."

His words—and his gaze—stole her breath. He was sincere. Evelyn looked down, smiling shyly. "Okay, let's not get carried away."

"I'm serious." He was.

She immediately blushed, and her stomach knotted with excitement.

He continued. "Listen, I know I'm not your usual type, but I hope when you've had enough time to heal, you'll consider going out with me again."

"Wow." Evelyn was stunned into silence. She had been utterly unprepared for this smart, gentle, funny guy to so bluntly tell her where he stood regarding their relationship. Especially so soon.

"So now that I've totally ruined this date and made it super awkward . . ." Will said sarcastically.

Laughing, Evelyn shook her head. "Not at all. I'm flattered. And surprised. You're different from what I thought you'd be."

"Is that a good thing?"

"Very good," she assured him, smiling. "And we'll definitely go out again."

The waitress came over to take their order, interrupting the moment. Evelyn wondered what else they might have said if they hadn't been cut off.

The two spent the next couple of hours sharing entrées as they got to know each other better. She learned he had been a band geek in high school and that he loved classic rock, just like she did. He shared with her that he'd lost his father when he was very young to a car accident and that he'd been helping his mother with bills and running the house since the moment he'd been old enough to get a job. Will was seemingly perfect, and she allowed herself to forget the time as she sat with him, losing herself in the conversation and in his emerald eyes.

"I'm having a really great time, Will. I needed a good night out with a guy who's sweet and respectful."

"I'm having fun, too," he responded shyly.

"I know I asked you out tonight, but I still think it's a good idea for me—and for you—if I move very carefully into anything new since I just got out of a pretty crazy relationship." She paused, trying to gauge his facial expression. He was unfazed.

"I totally agree." He reached for his napkin. "I like you, Evelyn. But I'm not rushing you into a single thing. If you want to be friends, let's do that. Let's build slowly. I'm okay with whatever you need."

She hadn't expected such a calm, rational reaction. "Thank you," she finally said quietly. "You have no idea what that means to me right now." She put her hand on his. "I like you, too. And I think we should have more nights just like this. Spend time together and get to know each other more."

"I'm one hundred percent on board with that. You set the pace. I'm not going anywhere."

At that moment she knew they were headed toward something worth waiting for and that Will was meant to be in her life for a reason. She was ready to wait as long as it took to find out exactly why.

Chapter 21
2003

One month later

Evelyn glanced behind her at Will as she unlocked her apartment. He waited patiently as she fiddled with the keys and door handle, standing back to give her some room. He did so many little things to make her comfortable, and she wondered if he knew how much she appreciated them. It had been about a month since their initial date, but this was Will's first time at Evelyn's apartment. He had never even asked to come up. He'd shown nothing but patience and compassion as she'd worked on healing from everything that had happened with Cole.

"Sorry for the mess." She picked up a stray cardigan from the back of her armchair.

"What mess?" Will asked, motioning to the clean room. "I wish my place looked like this when I came home late at night!"

She headed back into the kitchen to grab them each a bottle of water from the fridge. "So, what should we do?"

He was unsure what to say as he accepted his bottle from across the kitchen island, and it occurred to her that she might have inferred something she hadn't meant to.

She quickly corrected herself. "Wanna watch a movie?"

His shoulders relaxed. "Sure!" he said, making his way to her collection of DVDs under the TV.

As she watched him thumb through the options, it struck her for the millionth time that week how cute he was and how endearing it was that he seemed just as nervous about being in her apartment for the first time as she was. She was secure with him. He wasn't trying to be smooth, and he wasn't controlling. He was nice. And not in the way she'd normally use the word to describe someone who was otherwise not her type, but in the way that made him the type of guy she'd marry someday.

The weeks they'd spent getting to know each other had been nothing short of perfect, and Evelyn couldn't help but fall for him in spite of her own request to take things slowly, which Will had taken seriously. Not once had he pressured her into doing anything she wasn't ready for. He'd followed her lead, communicating with her openly about what she needed along the way. It was the opposite of what she'd experienced with Cole, and being with Will was refreshing and fun. He'd met Cammie and passed her rigorous screening with flying colors, turning Cammie into Will's biggest fan. Evelyn loved spending time with her best friend and her boyfriend at the same time.

"Wait, you're a Mel Brooks fan?" he asked, excitedly holding up her copy of *Blazing Saddles*.

Evelyn snapped out of her musings to answer. "That's one of my favorite movies of all time," she said, sitting on the couch and grabbing the TV remote. "I could probably recite the entire thing by heart."

"Done and done!" Will inserted the disc into the player. "I have literally never met a girl who actually likes this movie." He beamed at her as he sat down near her, careful not to touch her. He was shy, and she liked that. She had been so controlled during her relationship with Cole she'd forgotten what it was like to be on a couch with a person who was calm and easygoing.

Will picked up the DVD remote and clicked through the menu to play the movie. As they laughed together at the same jokes, she shifted her body closer to him and tucked her feet under her, her knee touching his upper thigh. It was a small move, but she hoped he'd receive it. She gauged the reaction on his face. He smiled and rested his hand gently on her knee. She smiled back and settled into the couch, pulling her legs out from under her and allowing their bodies to lean against each other as they watched. After a few minutes, to Evelyn's delight, he reached his arm behind her and pulled her closer.

"Is this okay?"

"It's definitely okay," she whispered, touched that he'd asked.

She rested her head on his shoulder, unable to keep the smile off her face as the butterflies in her stomach swarmed.

They sat like that for a long time. Eventually, Evelyn got up to retrieve her slippers from her bedside. "I'll be right back." By habit, she walked straight to her desk and moved her mouse to make her screen saver go away so she could check her IM messages. She had a few, but there was one name on the list that was like a punch to the gut when she saw it. Cole's.

They hadn't spoken in weeks, and his username on her screen chilled her to the bone. She debated whether to open his message or just close her laptop and try to put it out of her mind so she could carry on her night with Will. Her curiosity got the best of her, and she clicked the message open.

It read simply, "Check your email." Hesitantly, she opened her email and clicked on Cole's untitled message. Her heart dropped.

The email contained pictures of her having dinner with Will at Hearth a month ago. And a long rant from an obviously drunk Cole, cursing at her, calling her names, and threatening to murder both Evelyn and Will. She held back tears as she read. He knew exactly how to hurt her and what buttons to push, and he did it well. She was angry that someone had been following her around, taking photos of her while she was out, violating her privacy. Cole's message was especially jarring in this of all moments when she finally felt safe and protected. She let out an audible sob, clapping her hand over her mouth to stop it.

"Hey, you okay?"

Evelyn's head whipped toward the door.

Will peeked into the room, concerned. "Sorry, I heard crying."

"I'm okay. It's—" she didn't know what to say, so she went with the truth. "I got these really scary messages from Cole, and I just . . . Here, look!" She gestured toward her laptop as she spoke.

Will walked over, leaning down to read the message Cole had sent. His brows furrowed in confusion when he clicked on the photos. "Wait, are these from Hearth?" he asked. "Is that us?"

"Yes! I have no idea how he got them or how he knew we were out together, but now he's freaking out because he's jealous!"

"It's been a month! Why does he care if we had dinner weeks ago?"

"Because he's a *psycho*, Will!" she exclaimed, waving her hands in exasperation. "He doesn't want me to be with anyone if it's not him!" She paused, realizing she'd inadvertently pulled Will into her messy situation with Cole and that he probably didn't want any part of this. "Ugh." She put her head in her hands. "I'm so sorry I got you wrapped up in this. Now he's mad at *you*, and you didn't even do anything."

"Whatever. He can be mad," Will said nonchalantly. "What's he gonna do to me?"

"Honestly, Will, that's what I'm afraid of! I don't trust him!"

"Okay, listen, tell me this." He placed his hands on her shoulders and looked her in the eye. "Do you think—like *honestly* think—he would come here and try something? Tonight?"

"I don't know! I don't know what he's gonna do. He's obviously drunk, and I'm scared! Not just for me, but I don't want him coming after you!"

"He's not coming after anyone," Will said, standing squarely in front of her, his hands still cradling her shoulders gently. "I'm gonna stay here tonight in case he shows up. I'll crash on the couch, okay?"

Evelyn's first instinct was to refuse. She was so programmed by Cole to deny any and all advances from men, even innocent or platonic ones. Still, she wanted Will to stay. Not necessarily for fun, but he made her feel protected, and she definitely didn't want to be alone.

"Are you sure?"

"Let's go finish the movie," he said, closing her laptop. He led her back to the living room, and they sat down on the couch once more. He pulled her close, and she rested her head on his shoulder as he pushed play.

She snuggled in closer to him, happy he was there. He had a way of calming her that she'd never experienced with anyone before. She wanted him to kiss her, but he was waiting for her to make that move, and it suited her just fine. They cuddled and watched the movie until nearly the end, when sleepiness crept over her.

At one point, she snapped her head up, startling Will. "Sorry." She smiled sleepily. "I almost dozed off on your shoulder."

"Don't apologize." He grinned. "Let's get you to bed."

Evelyn's heart jumped. Was he propositioning her? It wasn't like him to be so direct, but she also didn't think she'd say no if he was. She stood up with him and allowed him to lead her into the bedroom.

He turned down her comforter and switched off the main light, flicking on her bedside lamp. He motioned for her to get into bed. She complied, curious to find out where this was going. Will pulled the comforter up over her body to her waist as she sat up in bed, then he left the room. He quickly returned with a glass of water from the kitchen, placing it on the bedside table.

"Need anything else?"

"No, I don't think so," she said coyly.

"Get some sleep. I'll be out there." He gently moved her hair out of her eye and tucked it behind her ear. It was such a tender touch, and not the type she was used to. She reached up and held his hand, and their eyes locked.

"You're very sweet, you know that?"

He leaned forward and pressed his lips against hers, lingering for a few seconds before pulling back and turning out the lamp. "Goodnight," he whispered, leaving the room. She couldn't wipe the smile from her face as she pressed her head into her pillow, her body swirling with adrenaline.

He rustled around in the living room as he got comfortable on the couch. The screen flickered as he channel surfed. Evelyn was falling head over heels for this kind soul who had come so unexpectedly into her life. He seemed too good to be true, which in itself raised a little red flag in Evelyn's mind. In her experience, men who seemed too good to be true usually were. But for now, she was happy. Totally safe for the first time in days, Evelyn fell into a deep, sound sleep that took her decades away from Will and back to her other life.

Chapter 22

1919

The October air was chilly as Thomas and Evelyn walked toward Dr. Holstead's house. It had taken him a few weeks to track down the address, and Evelyn was both anxious and excited to finally meet the doctor and find out if he had any answers for them about her dreams. Her jaw was clenched tightly, and several times she failed to answer Thomas, her head swimming with possibilities.

"Nervous?" Thomas asked.

"A bit. I just hope it's all right, popping up at this poor man's door bothering him after he's been retired all these years."

"Let me handle the doc." He smiled. "I know how to work these professor types."

Evelyn scoffed at him. "Be my guest."

Thomas checked the address he'd written down and matched it with the numbers on the building in front of them. "We're here."

They climbed the porch stairs of the ornate row house, and Thomas knocked on the door. Soon, an elderly woman answered, raising her eyebrows at the young couple.

"Good afternoon, ma'am," Thomas said. "My name is Thomas Allen. I'm a doctoral candidate over at NYU. I work with some people who know your husband, Dr. Holstead?"

The woman laughed. "Husband? Oh no, Dr. Holstead is not my husband. I work for him. I'm his caregiver, Ms. Brooks."

"I'm so sorry," Thomas said, embarrassed at his mistake.

"It happens all the time!" The woman beamed. "What do you want with the doctor?"

"Well, I'm working on a particular topic of study in which I believe Dr. Holstead was an important part, and I was hoping I might pick his brain a bit. For my research," Thomas said.

Evelyn was impressed. He was a better liar than she'd expected.

"Dr. Holstead doesn't get many visitors these days, but I'll ask him if he's up to it. Come in." Ms. Brooks ushered them inside.

"Thank you," Thomas said. "We'll only be a minute. It would really help my thesis."

Ms. Brooks smiled, glancing at Evelyn. "I'll go and see if he's ready for company." She turned, disappearing down the hallway.

Evelyn and Thomas flashed amused grins at each other, silent. He shrugged as she eyed him. "What?" he whispered, laughing quietly. "I told you I'd handle it."

Just then, Ms. Brooks appeared from around the corner. "The doctor will be with you in a minute. Come, let's go into the sitting room." She led Evelyn and Thomas into a small room off the hallway where they sat in two armchairs next to each other.

"Would either of you like anything to drink? Tea?"

"No, thank you," Evelyn said quickly. "We won't be long."

A slight figure appeared in the doorway. "And who do we have here, Ms. Brooks?" Dr. Holstead shuffled into the room and approached Evelyn and Thomas.

"This is Mr. Thomas Allen, a doctoral student at the university. He wanted to ask you some questions about some of your work," Ms. Brooks said. "And this is—" She gestured to Evelyn. "I'm afraid I didn't get your name, dear."

"Evelyn Moore. Mr. Allen and I are friends."

"I see," Dr. Holstead replied. "Nice to meet you."

"You as well. I hope we haven't come at an inconvenient time."

"I'm old, retired, and bored," Holstead clipped back with a smile. "All I have is time!" The old man laughed at his own joke. "What can I help you two with today?"

"Well, Doctor, a big part of my research is focused on dreaming and the different ways people experience their dreams," Thomas said. "I found your name in this fascinating book, and I just had to ask you some questions."

Taking the book from Thomas, Dr. Holstead gazed at it, turning it over slowly. "I didn't know anyone had actually ever read this," he muttered. "The research here is mostly complete. What could you possibly have left to ask?"

"This whole book is written by Dr. Fletcher. You're barely in it anywhere. But the two of you were partners for many years, weren't you?"

"We were," Holstead said matter-of-factly.

"So if you were partners, why are you not listed as a co-author?" Thomas asked, confused.

"Because I didn't write the book. I didn't even want the book written in the first place!" Holstead tossed the book onto his desk. "I did all the research alongside Fletch, but I wanted out of the whole thing before he ever wrote a word of it."

Furrowing her brow in confusion, Evelyn couldn't help but chime in. "But why?" she asked.

The old man's knuckles turned white as he gripped the arms of his chair, deep in thought. "I needed to get away."

"You mean you wanted to retire?" Thomas asked.

"No, no." Holstead shook his head as he answered. "I just hated watching what the dreams did to all those poor people in the end."

Evelyn stiffened. Glancing at her, Thomas replied. "To what people? The dreamers?"

"Yes!" said Holstead. "The dreams were a gift until they were a curse, and they *always* ended up a curse."

Evelyn's mouth was suddenly dry, and her head started spinning. She regretted not taking Ms. Brooks up on the offer of a beverage.

"Could you possibly elaborate on what you mean by that?" asked Thomas, trying to sound even-keeled and neutral. He could sense Evelyn's panic and tried to keep the focus on himself. "What ended up happening to them ultimately?"

Dr. Holstead sighed deeply as if preparing himself to relive a particularly bad memory. "It killed them," he said blankly, staring at the floor. "All of them."

Chapter 23
1919

Evelyn thought she might faint in the middle of Holstead's sitting room. She deliberately inhaled and exhaled as Thomas spoke to Dr. Holstead. Her ears were ringing, and the blood drained from her face the second Dr. Holstead mentioned the dreamers dying. She reached into her bag for her handkerchief, using it to dab her forehead which was suddenly cold with sweat.

"Are you all right, my dear?"

Evelyn snapped back to reality as Dr. Holstead addressed her. She had trouble coming up with an appropriate response. She wasn't all right.

"You've gone awfully pale," said Holstead, concerned. "Are you quite healthy?"

Thomas, realizing Evelyn was struggling, jumped in as he walked over to her. "She's fine," he said, grabbing her shoulders gently. His hands were warm on her upper arms. "Ms. Moore hasn't eaten much today."

Dr. Holstead reached over to the side table next to the settee and rang a small bell, summoning Ms. Brooks. "Let's get you something to eat!"

Ms. Brooks appeared in the doorway shortly, and Dr. Holstead asked her politely to fetch Evelyn a snack. Poor Ms. Brooks was on a fool's errand. Evelyn wasn't hungry. She was completely terrified. She had to keep up the act, though, to get any useful information from this visit, so she gratefully nibbled on some cookies arranged on a small plate as the men began discussing the dreamers once more.

"I'm afraid I don't quite understand," Thomas said. "How exactly did dreams kill the subjects?"

"Well, you can't be in two places at once." Holstead shrugged. "So the universe . . . corrected itself."

"You mean the time travel part?" Thomas asked.

"Precisely," Holstead answered, leaning forward. "Eventually, we must all end up in just one place, at one time. The dreamers were able to go back and forth in a way no one else could, but it caught up with them."

"So you're saying all the dreamers in your study got, what? Exhausted? From time traveling?"

"In a sense," said Holstead. He scooted closer to the edge of his seat and began motioning with his hands as he spoke. "Imagine a candle. Whenever you light it, the wick burns and the wax melts, making the candle shorter, understand?" Dr. Holstead paused to make sure Thomas was following.

Thomas nodded, prompting Holstead to continue.

"With the dreamers, think of the wick as the human brain and the wax as the body. As they traveled back and forth every night their entire lives, their wicks burned quickly, their bodies—the wax—more slowly over time, changing its shape and makeup as the wick burned."

Thomas glanced at Evelyn, making sure she was okay. Taking a sip of her tea, Evelyn listened intently, trying to stay calm and quiet as Holstead continued. Inside, she was buzzing with a million emotions. Holstead had just confirmed she was actually a time traveler, and both her lives were real. Neither life and none of her loves had been a dream. It was a lot to take in while maintaining her composure. She wished they could leave so she could talk to Thomas about it.

"So you see," said Holstead, "at some point, the body changes so much that it can no longer function. The wick must stop burning. Unfortunately, humans are not candles, and when our wicks stop burning, we die."

Evelyn swallowed the lump in her throat and willed her voice to hold as she spoke. "Do they die in both their lives?" she asked, almost whispering.

"No. The dreamers all lost only one of their timelines. They didn't know which one it would be until it started happening."

"So, if I understand correctly, you're saying people who time travel in their dreams, like the ones in your study, they just . . . pass away in one life? And keep living in their other timelines?" Evelyn asked.

"In a nutshell, yes," Holstead confirmed. "The dreamers who stopped dreaming stayed alive here, but some did not handle the loss of their dream lives well."

When Evelyn dropped her handkerchief out of her shaky hand and onto the floor, Thomas took over the conversation, giving her a moment to catch her breath. "And what signs were there that the dreamers were losing one of their lives?" he asked.

"The ones we saw pass away in this timeline experienced blackout spells, dizziness. Some experienced forgetfulness and heightened emotions. These would present for a while before the dreamer ultimately transitioned full-time to . . . wherever they went in their dreams, I suppose."

"Makes sense." Thomas tried to read Evelyn's face. He wished he had come alone. She was understandably having a hard time hearing all this and keeping her cool. "It's getting late," he said. "I should get Ms. Moore home before dark."

Evelyn was exhausted and overloaded with information but still wanted to know more. She hoped they could come back soon. Thomas was already standing, and Dr. Holstead was headed toward the door. She placed her teacup and saucer on the table next to her chair and joined Thomas in saying goodbye to the doctor, who rang the bell to beckon Ms. Brooks to walk his guests out.

"I hope you won't mind if I reach back out at some point," Thomas said to Holstead. "I'm sure I'll have some more questions about the dreamers as my research progresses."

"Anytime, my boy," the doctor answered happily. He seemed invigorated at the idea of his work being useful. "I'm not sure I can be of much help, but I'd be delighted to assist you."

"Thank you for your time, Doctor." Evelyn smiled politely. "It was so good of you to speak with us this evening. And a pleasure to meet you."

"And you as well, Ms. Moore." Holstead beamed back at her. "I do hope you'll take in a hearty meal when you arrive home."

Evelyn laughed, embarrassed. "I will."

Ms. Brooks came in and handed Thomas and Evelyn their coats. "Get home safely," she said as she bustled them out the front door.

Thanking her, Evelyn and Thomas descended the porch stairs and began their stroll toward her apartment.

Once they were far enough away, Evelyn broke the silence. "I'm going to die, Thomas."

He stopped in his tracks, turning to face her. "Listen to me. You are not going anywhere. I'm gonna figure this out!" His jaw was set, and his eyes were ablaze.

His graveness surprised her but did little to convince her of his words. "Do you think there's actually a way to stop it?" Her shoulders sagged with the weight of her hopelessness.

"I don't know, but if there is, I'm going to find it." The care in his voice touched her.

"You know you don't have to help me," she said. "This is a lot for someone you met just a few weeks ago."

Thomas cast his eyes down at the sidewalk briefly, pondering how to respond. Finally, he lifted his head and gently took her chin in his hand, tilting her face upward. "Evelyn, I don't know why, but I feel like I've known you for way longer than a few weeks, and I would be lying if I said I wasn't falling for you." She took a sharp breath in as he spoke, his warm hand still softly cupping her chin. "I want you to stay here so I can keep falling," he said. "I'm gonna figure this out. Trust me."

Evelyn didn't know how to answer. She fought the urge to collapse into his arms right there in the middle of the city. "I trust you," she said, almost whispering. "I trust you."

The two walked, arms linked, back to Evelyn's apartment building. They didn't talk. They didn't need to. When they arrived outside the entrance, Evelyn longed for him to stay, but it wasn't proper.

"I suppose this is goodnight," she said sadly. She needed him right now. She was scared after what Dr. Holstead had told them, and the thought of being alone made her uneasy. "Breakfast tomorrow? Meet me before work."

"I'll be outside your office building." He smiled, trying to lift the mood.

"Good evening, Thomas," Evelyn said, still holding his hands in hers, not wanting to let go.

"Good evening, Ms. Moore." The tension in the air between them was thick. She turned to walk inside, every step away harder than the last. The second she was in the elevator and out of his view, she already missed him.

Evelyn went about her evening, all the while replaying in her mind what Dr. Holstead had said. She had to know more. Which life would end? How long did she have? How would she know when the symptoms started? Could she sleep less in one of her lives and delay whatever would eventually happen to her? She reminded herself to trust Thomas and curled up on her bed, hugging a pillow close to her chest. Afraid to fall asleep, Evelyn reached into her nightstand drawer and pulled out a handful of dream journals she'd already filled. Opening one, she began reading, searching for clues in her own dreams that might provide answers. She didn't find anything helpful, but she did stumble upon an entry she'd written when she was much younger.

I almost brought up my dreams to Mother today. I had a really great one last night where I went on a weekend trip to New York City with my dream family. I wanted to tell Mother about how different the city looks in the future and about the underground trains and how much taller all the buildings are. But I knew she'd go mad and say I was making things up again, so I didn't tell her. I hate not being able to talk to her or Father about my dream life. They don't know me very well. Half of me is a secret.

Evelyn's heart ached for the little girl who'd written that entry, especially now after visiting Holstead. Her parents had made her feel so guilty about her dreams her entire life, and she wished she could talk to them right now and tell them they were wrong. But she couldn't talk to anyone except Thomas, at least not yet. She still didn't have all the answers. She scoured the pages of the journals until she could no longer keep her eyes open. Lying among a pile of books, she eventually rested her head on her arm and went back to Will.

Chapter 24
2003

Evelyn awoke with a start to Will tapping lightly on her bedroom door. She sat up, trying to make sense of him being in her apartment and everything she and Thomas had just discovered in her dreams. After a few groggy moments, Evelyn recalled that Will had spent the night and why. Her heart sank as she remembered Cole and his threatening messages.

"Thank you for staying," she said, attempting to straighten her hair and wipe any stray eyeliner from under her eyes. This was the first time Will had ever seen her without her hair and makeup done properly. "I'm glad Cole didn't end up coming by. I was nervous."

"You're welcome," he said, sitting on the edge of the bed. "You okay?"

She nodded and smiled reassuringly. She didn't want to tell him what she'd found out about the dreamers yet. Things were going so well between them, and she didn't want to freak him out. He'd already been understanding about so many odd things. "Do you want to get some breakfast?"

"Sure," Will said. "I can run down and grab us some bagels from the deli if you want."

"Let's both go," Evelyn said, sliding out of bed. "I could use some fresh air."

"Are you sure? I don't want Cole stalking us during breakfast," he pointed out.

"Cole will not stop me from having a bagel with you," Evelyn said, rummaging through her dresser for some jeans.

"Fair enough!" Will laughed as he walked out of the bedroom and shut the door to give her some privacy.

A few minutes later, the two were walking briskly down the block to the bagel shop Evelyn frequented. She tried to put the information from Dr.

Holstead out of her mind so she could focus on Will, making as much small talk as she could as they headed to get breakfast.

"I hope you'll still want to hang out with me after last night," she half-joked. Cole's threats might make Will think twice about pursuing her further.

"Why wouldn't I?" Will seemed genuinely confused.

"Well, I'm sure ex-boyfriend drama wasn't on the list of traits you were looking for in a girlfriend," she said, embarrassed she'd just called herself his girlfriend out loud.

"Um, you time travel in your sleep." Will laughed, undeterred by her use of the title. "I can handle ex-boyfriend drama." He paused before saying, "I'm happy to deal with it if that's the price of spending more time with you."

Her stomach flipped in that now-familiar way. He was good at that. They arrived at the bagel shop, saving her from coming up with a clever response. She said a silent thank you to the universe for not bumping them into Cole on the way there.

Once she'd ordered and sat down, Evelyn searched for the right thing to say to Will. Holstead's news was still lurking in the back of her mind. She tried to shake it off. "So, how uncomfortable was my couch?" she asked.

"My back will recover in about a week." He dramatically stretched and made a show of cracking his spine.

She laughed. "I should have offered you the bed. I feel bad. Not very good hostessing on my part," she said as a barista brought their drinks over to the table.

"I wouldn't have let you," Will said, removing the lid from his coffee to allow the steam to escape.

"Such a gentleman." She sipped her hot tea.

"I just want you to be comfortable."

Evelyn studied his face, noting the kindness and sincerity in his eyes. She really could see herself taking Will back home to meet her parents someday. He was everything a father would want for his daughter. Polite, respectful, smart, and protective. She couldn't let him get away.

"I didn't want you to leave last night, you know," she said, reclining in her chair, her cup in both hands.

"I didn't want to leave you, either. Not after those creepy messages from Cole."

"No, I mean I didn't want you to leave *regardless* of the messages from Cole," Evelyn admitted. "I wanted you to stay before that."

"If you'd asked me to stay, I would have said yes."

They both leaned forward and entwined their fingers. "Let's go on another dinner date, but this time let's go somewhere we can't be photographed by Cole's paparazzi." She grinned.

"Let's do it," Will said, releasing her hand to make space for the bagels the barista had just delivered. "I'll think of a safe place for us to go. When are you free?"

"The sooner the better."

"Agreed." He smiled. "How about tomorrow? I have no afternoon classes."

"I'm done at three!" Evelyn's heart fluttered. She glanced around the room, nervous that something—or someone—would ruin the moment. "Hey, you wanna get outta here? We can eat at my place."

"Actually, I should probably get back home," Will said, standing up. "I have to meet with my group from bio for a project this afternoon."

"Gotcha," she said, trying to hide her disappointment. "I should probably get some studying done, too, now that you mention it."

"I'll walk you back home." Will put on his coat and gathered his bagel and coffee.

Will took her hand in his, and the two strolled. Evelyn scanned her surroundings every now and then, worried Cole or one of his friends would be lurking around the next corner. She tried to convince herself there was nothing to worry about. That Cole had been drunk when he'd sent those messages. She focused on Will, trying to savor her last moments with him before he had to go.

When they arrived in the lobby of her building, Will walked Evelyn to the elevator. She stared at the floor, sad to be parting from him.

"Hey, what's up?" he asked.

"I don't want you to go," Evelyn mumbled, embarrassed. "I like it when you're with me."

"I like it when I'm with you, too." He pulled her close, and they hugged for a long time before prying themselves apart.

"I'm gonna push the elevator button now, so I *have* to force myself to leave you and go meet my group," Will said.

"No!" She laughed, playfully smacking his hand away from the button. He pushed it anyway, and she hugged him again, knowing time was almost up. "I'm excited for tomorrow," she said, her words muffled in his jacket.

"Me, too," He kissed the top of her head softly. The elevator dinged, and the door slid open. It was empty. She looked up at him, and he immediately kissed her. As the doors began to close, they parted lips, and he held the elevator open so she could get in. "I'll see you tomorrow."

The doors closed, and Evelyn leaned against the wall and shut her eyes, absolutely ecstatic at how things with Will were going. She straightened herself up and marched out of the elevator, fishing for her keys in her jacket pocket. Inside her apartment, Evelyn sat down at her desk in the bedroom and unwrapped her bagel, flipping open her laptop. She'd been so distracted by Will all morning that she hadn't even thought about Holstead and what he'd said about the dreamers.

Evelyn stared at her computer screen as she remembered what the other dreamers' fate might mean for her. She wondered what had happened to their other lives when they died. Had they lost one or both of their worlds, ultimately? She had so many questions. The more her mind reeled, the more emotional Evelyn became. She ran through the possibilities.

She could die here *and* in her other life and be gone from both worlds, leaving Will and Thomas. And her parents. And Mr. Allen. And her friends. Her breath caught in her throat at the idea of just being *gone*. It was so final.

Another possibility was that she would die sometime here in this life and live on in her earlier life forever. Or she could die there and live here forever. Would she be able to slow it down or stop it, or would the whole thing be out of her hands? She needed to know more. She had to get Thomas back to Holstead for more answers. Soon.

Evelyn finished half the bagel, gulped down some of her now-cold tea, and took a shower. She couldn't sleep yet, as much as she wanted to go back to 1919 and find out more about her time traveling dreams. It was only noon. Distracting herself the rest of the day by IM'ing Cammie to gush about Will and gossip about Cole's scary messages the night before, Evelyn procrastinated her studying until it was almost dark. She finally took out her books, scolding herself for waiting so long. She sat down on her bed and got to work. After a few hours, she put her books aside and cleaned up her bed. She walked into the living room and grabbed the blanket Will had used the night before. Bringing it into her bedroom, she wrapped herself up in it and closed her eyes. Swooning over Will, Evelyn drifted off to 1919 to find Thomas and, she hoped, some more answers.

Chapter 25
1919

Evelyn had an extra bounce in her step as she hurried to meet Thomas. She couldn't help but be charmed by him even though she could tell he wasn't necessarily trying to charm her. He was easy to read. He liked her, and he hadn't made a mystery of it. In spite of not knowing him long, he'd given her something she'd been seeking since moving to New York: a partner.

She and Thomas shared similar interests and had spent time over the last few weeks doing things together outside of digging for answers about her dreams. She found herself at ease, always her true self in his company. It was something she wasn't used to, which Evelyn blamed on her own historically poor taste in men.

She spied Thomas leaning against her building, reading. She quickened her pace, eager to get to him. Thomas smiled as her shadow darkened the pages of his book. He closed it and greeted her with a peck on the cheek and a warm grin.

"I hope I didn't interrupt anything too riveting," Evelyn said, tapping the cover of his book.

"Actually," Thomas said, holding the book up so she could read the title on the spine, "I'm doing some more digging into your dream situation." He gestured toward a nearby path. "Shall we walk?"

Side by side, Evelyn and Thomas made their way through the park, and he elaborated on what he'd learned from his book.

"I hope you don't mind, but I took the liberty of doing a little more research about things related to time travel. I thought perhaps it might be helpful while we wait for Holstead to give us more information," he said.

"Not at all," Evelyn answered. "In fact, if you hadn't done it already, I might have asked you to." She paused, her face falling. She stopped walking and turned to him. "I'm getting really scared, Thomas."

"I know." His tone somehow made her a little less terrified. "We're going to figure this out. I promise."

"I just wish I knew *when* it would happen, or how I would recognize it had started," she said, the desperation making her voice shake slightly. "I hate knowing I could just suddenly start fading away someday and there's nothing I can do to stop it."

"Let's take it one step at a time," Thomas said. "Nothing has happened *yet*. Let's try to get ahead of it."

Evelyn sighed. He was so sure he could help her, but she wasn't so certain. The idea of having to unravel this whole mystery seemed extremely daunting. Anger rose in her chest. She despised not knowing if she should even pursue a future with him. "What if we can't figure it out?" she asked, her eyes welling with tears.

"Listen, I get that it's scary. I don't know how you've managed to stay so strong after finding out all this stuff about the dreamers. But I swear I will do everything I can to make sure you're safe, do you hear me?" Fire flashed in his eyes as he spoke.

He genuinely cared about her. It was as if she was falling in love with a lifelong friend. Evelyn took Thomas's hand in her own and squeezed it before letting go.

"I believe you," she said. "I do."

"Good." He stared at her intently. "It's going to be all right, Evelyn. You know that, don't you?"

Shaking her head slowly, Evelyn scoffed. "I honestly *don't* know that it will be. But I'm relieved to have you with me, no matter how it goes."

"I'm glad, too." They stared into each other's eyes for what seemed like ages. She wished they weren't in public. Evelyn wanted nothing more than for him to kiss her. She knew he wouldn't, but the idea made the butterflies in her stomach flutter. As if sensing her desires, Thomas lifted Evelyn's hands to his mouth and tenderly kissed her fingertips.

After a few more moments of silence, the pair carried on their walk.

"My mother asked if you'd like to come for dinner again, by the way." He chuckled at his mother's well-meaning meddling.

"I can't tonight, actually," she lamented. "I'm meeting Calvin after work to break things off for good." Evelyn twisted her face in disgust, causing Thomas to laugh. Over the last few weeks, Evelyn had put Calvin off a few times, feigning illness and lying about having other plans every time he'd asked her out. She knew she had to tell him she wasn't interested, but she hadn't been ready to upset another volatile man.

"Ah, finally breaking poor Cal's heart!" he joked, calling Calvin the wrong name on purpose.

"It's not funny!" She laughed, playfully smacking his arm. "I don't *enjoy* breaking up with people. He is just . . . not right. For me, I mean."

"I have to agree." Thomas smiled.

They walked to Evelyn's office, laughing and joking the whole way. His humor and warmth made her forget all her troubles for those few blocks. Before he left, she grabbed his arm.

"Thomas, please, try and set up a meeting with Dr. Holstead as soon as you can," Evelyn pleaded. "I don't want to rush him, but I really do need some more answers."

"I promise," he said. "I'll let you know as soon as I can." Squeezing Evelyn's hand one last time, Thomas turned and left.

Evelyn entered the lobby of her office building, basking in the afterglow of her morning with him. She raised her eyes to greet the elevator attendant and stopped dead in her tracks when instead Calvin stood looming in front of her.

She gasped. "Calvin! What are you doing here?" Evelyn plastered the most genuine smile she could across her face, trying to cover up her shock—and dismay—at seeing him, hoping he hadn't seen her with Thomas a few moments before.

"Better question," Calvin said flatly, "is what were *you* doing out *there*?" He gestured toward the sidewalk through the lobby doors.

Her stomach dropped. He had seen them.

"I was just coming from a walk with a friend," Evelyn said a little louder than she'd intended. "He's my boss's nephew. We were discussing books."

"Books?" He scoffed. "Looks to me like you've been doing more than just talking about books since I last saw you."

His agitation at her recent behavior was understandable but didn't excuse his rudeness. The elevator attendant had disappeared to take someone up, and no one else was in sight.

Suddenly, he snatched her upper arm and dragged her around the corner into a nook of mailboxes, causing her to stumble slightly. Once he was satisfied they were out of sight, he got so close to her face she could feel his breath. She backed up until her back hit the mailboxes, causing the metal panels to rattle loudly.

"You will *not* make a fool of me!" he snapped. "You've been avoiding me for weeks and now I see you with someone else? I won't have any girl of mine ignoring me and traipsing around the city with some skinny nobody making me look bad! Do you hear me?"

Evelyn didn't know what to say. His strength overpowered her, forcing her to shrink the way she had when the gunman forced her to slide her back down the wall. To cower the way she had when Cole attacked her. Just as she opened her mouth to scream, a voice came from around the corner.

"Hey! Get away from her!"

Evelyn and Calvin whipped their heads toward the voice. Her knees went weak when she saw Thomas, wide-eyed and ready for a fight, the book he'd been carrying thoughtlessly discarded onto the floor nearby.

"Thomas!" she cried, running to him as Calvin stepped back from her. Thomas pushed her behind him, shielding her from Calvin.

Calvin flashed a menacing grin as he approached them.

"I said stay away from her!" Thomas stiffened his stance as he spoke to Calvin, who clearly outweighed him. Evelyn didn't like the direction this was going. Calvin stopped in front of Thomas with their chests almost touching.

Just as Calvin was about to speak, two women turned into the nook to fetch their office mail. Evelyn breathed a sigh of relief as Calvin softened his frame, backed off, and pretended he hadn't been about to knock Thomas out cold. "You're lucky this time," he whispered, leaning in close to Thomas's ear while he looked straight at Evelyn. "Your luck will run out, I can promise you *both* that."

Patting Thomas hard on the back, Calvin straightened and walked out of the building.

Thomas turned to Evelyn, grabbing her face in his hands to check for any signs of damage. "Are you all right?"

"I'm fine," she said. "I'm so glad you were here!"

"I forgot to tell you something, so I came back, and I heard the mailboxes banging! Are you sure you're all right?" he said breathlessly as he pushed the hair out of her eyes and examined her again.

"I'm okay, really. Thank you for stepping in."

"You know I'd kill him before I'd let him do anything to hurt you," Thomas snarled. "Who does he think he is putting his hands on you like that?"

The two women emerged from the mail nook, headed for the elevator. Evelyn squeezed Thomas's arm, trying to calm him down. "Are *you* all right?"

Thomas took a deep breath, attempting to level himself.

"I'm fine." He exhaled. Once he gathered himself, he continued. "Listen, the reason I came back is because I forgot to mention something important about the dreams." He retrieved the book from the floor where it had landed. "I don't know if you can control your dreams much, or at all," he said, "but I think it would be helpful if maybe, in your dreams—in

2003—you research any of the dreamers from Holstead and Fletcher's study who traveled to the future. Find out if there's any more information about how they died. Maybe we can learn something from them. Maybe you could even find one of them and talk to them!"

Evelyn was impressed that he'd thought of it and irritated with herself for not thinking of it sooner.

He continued. "Check their death records, obituaries, whatever you think might be helpful. It could tell us more about how to stop this whole thing from happening to you."

"Great idea," Evelyn said. "I'll let you know if I find anything."

"All right." Thomas wanted to usher Evelyn back into the mailbox nook for a quick kiss but thought better of it given what had just happened. Instead, he walked her to the elevator, handing her off to the attendant. "Please escort Ms. Moore safely to her office," Thomas asked him politely. He turned to Evelyn. "Are you all right from here?"

"I'm fine, thank you." She smiled at him in admiration. "I'll see you again soon, I hope."

"You will," he said. "Good day."

She watched him leave as the elevator doors shut and tried to hide the smile spreading across her face.

"He seems very nice, Ms. Moore." The attendant smiled. "Shall I walk you to your office?"

"That would be lovely," Evelyn answered. The walk wasn't far, and she thanked him as she entered, closing the door behind her. She hung her coat and set up her desk for the day as she thought over her eventful morning.

"Well, I guess Calvin knows we're done," she said aloud, rolling her eyes.

Her thoughts immediately turned to Thomas. He'd been so quick to step in when she was in danger. Calvin could easily have beat him senseless given the chance, but Thomas hadn't been intimidated by Calvin's size at all. All he'd thought about was protecting her. She remembered when Cole had stepped in front of a gunman for her. That moment had lost all the romance she'd previously wrapped it in when Cole attacked her, and she could no longer think of him as a hero. He was no better than the gunmen. It was impossible to picture Thomas ever putting his hands on her aggressively. He was too gentle and good. She considered the difference between Thomas's kind, genuine soul and Calvin's arrogant, materialistic motivations. She could draw the very same comparison between Will and Cole. It was impossible to ignore all the glaring parallels.

The office door clicking open jolted Evelyn out of her thoughts. Expecting her boss, she clapped her hand to her mouth when instead she saw Thomas's bloody and bruised face.

"What happened?" Evelyn cried, rushing around her desk to get to him. "Are you all right?"

"I ran into Calvin around the block," he said, wincing. "He ambushed me."

"Oh, Thomas, I am so sorry!" Guilt coursed through her veins. "I can't believe I got you involved in all this!" With her handkerchief, Evelyn carefully dabbed his swollen eye.

Sucking air through his teeth at the pain, Thomas tried to be still as Evelyn wiped the blood away. "Your boyfriend has a mean right hook."

"He is *not* my boyfriend," Evelyn snapped. "And if I ever run into him again, he'll be lucky if I don't give *him* a right hook."

Thomas couldn't help but laugh at the image. "I guess we'll have to be a little sneakier if we're going to spend time together."

The very idea boiled Evelyn's blood. She was tired of controlling, abusive men dictating who she could and couldn't spend time with. "You'll have to apply pressure to stop the bleeding." She removed the handkerchief from his brow. "How will you get home and avoid running into Cal?" she asked. She planned to use the name he hated from now on.

"I hadn't thought of that," he said.

"You should stay awhile, until we know it's safe."

"If you don't mind, that's probably the best thing. I'll try not to distract you from your work." He grinned mischievously, causing pain in his bruised eye.

"You can distract me anytime you like." Evelyn smiled. "At the very least, I owe you some aspirin."

"The spoils of war!" he retorted, making her laugh out loud.

She could get used to him being around.

Chapter 26

2003

Hunched over a stack of open books strewn across a large table at the campus library, Evelyn searched desperately for any information about the dreamers from Holstead and Fletcher's study. She wanted to follow Thomas's advice, but she was hitting one dead end after another. Admittedly, she was also having trouble focusing because, after the pictures Cole had sent of her and Will at dinner, she couldn't shake the fear Cole was going to pop up everywhere she went.

The spine of a medical journal crackled as she opened it, and she forced herself to focus. So far, she'd found a few fleeting references to Fletcher's book, though from what she could tell, his research had not made any waves in the world of psychology. Evelyn closed the book on top of the pile and sat back in her seat. Unsure of what she was missing, she shut her eyes and rocked back in her chair to think. When she opened her eyes, Will was standing in front of her flashing a cheeky grin. She'd told him a bit about Holstead and Fletcher's study and that she was searching for more information about the dreamers, but she'd intentionally not told him anything Holstead mentioned about the dreamers getting sick and dying. She needed more answers first.

Evelyn stood to greet him with a hug and a quick kiss.

"Anything good so far?" Will asked, sitting down next to her.

"Not much." She sighed with exasperation, sliding some books aside to make some room. "I must be looking in all the wrong places. I think I need a second set of less tired eyes."

"Have you tried the obits yet?" he asked, sifting through some of the books to catch himself up.

"Not yet," Evelyn said. "I figured I'd start by looking for studies that expanded on Fletcher and Holstead's. But as you can see . . ." She waved her hands at her mostly blank notepad and the stack of books on the table.

Will wanted desperately to help Evelyn solve this mystery so she could find some peace. "Okay, let's switch gears. Why don't we try to find articles about the dreamers? It doesn't have to be about the dreams. Look for anything with their names, like maybe they won a spelling bee or something and they made it into the local papers."

"Good call!" Evelyn exclaimed. She put her hand on his knee and squeezed it. "Thank you for helping me. This isn't exactly a fairy tale date."

Will laughed quietly. "I don't believe in fairy tales," he said, winking. "I'll take a good mystery over a fantasy any day, as long as I get my girl in the end."

"Oh, I'm pretty sure you're going to get her." After a few seconds of staring at each other, Evelyn stood up. "Wanna go solve this mystery?"

"Lead the way."

They went to the newspaper archives, and Will began to search the hometowns of the dreamers who'd time traveled to the late 1900s. They found nothing about the first few on the list, but when Evelyn searched for Caroline Huber, she jumped out of her seat.

"Will, look! I found Caroline!" she whispered excitedly. She beckoned for him to come over to her microfiche machine.

Will put his face close to the screen to read the old newspaper article Evelyn had found. "That is her!" he exclaimed a little too loudly for the library. He lowered his voice to a whisper. "That's her!"

They read over the article, Evelyn jotting everything down on her notepad. Caroline Huber's face stared back at them from the screen. She was sitting on a New York City street in handcuffs with a handful of other people, some Black and some White, at what appeared to be a protest of some sort. Evelyn read further and discovered Caroline had been arrested along with a group of other White protesters in 1964 when they'd demonstrated alongside Black parents against segregation.

Evelyn recalled Fletcher writing about Caroline's activism in the 1960s. "That matches up with what the book said about her."

"What happened to her after that?" Will wondered aloud. They walked back to the table where they had their laptops and the stacks of books from earlier. Evelyn typed Caroline's name into a search bar, followed by "New York." Scrolling the results, she found mentions of lots of Caroline Hubers, but none in New York, and none that matched the dates they had for Holstead and Fletcher's Caroline. A headline about a children's choir from upstate New York that won an award in a singing festival in 1995 caught Evelyn's eye. Their choir director was Caroline Huber. Based on the tiny thumbnail photo, Evelyn knew it was the same person from the photo in the '60s.

"Will!" she whispered. "Look!"

Will hurried over to Evelyn's side of the table. "That's definitely her," he agreed. A few minutes later, the library printer spat out information about Caroline's church. Evelyn grabbed the printout. "So, do we go find her? Try and talk to her?"

"Well, I would probably start by calling the church," Will said. "Ask if she still works there or whatever."

"This is why I keep you around!" She checked the time. "I'm exhausted. You wanna get outta here?"

"Love to," he answered, walking back to their table. "Wanna grab a bite to eat?"

"Yes, please!" Evelyn said, gathering the books to put them on the return cart. "I haven't eaten all day!"

They walked through a courtyard between several buildings toward the campus dining hall. They approached the door bantering about the questionable quality of the taco salad when Evelyn suddenly stopped in her tracks, a strange expression on her face. The world had started spinning.

"What's up?" Will asked, concerned.

She stared ahead, a blank expression in her eyes.

"Evelyn?"

Fuzzy swirls that vaguely resembled the campus buildings spiraled all around her.

Suddenly, her knees gave out, and she crumpled to the ground, half conscious. Will tried to catch her, but it was too late.

"What is happening?!" he cried.

A few bystanders had gathered, and a girl asked if he needed any help.

"I don't know. I don't know what's wrong with her!" Will said, frantic. "Evelyn, talk to me!" She was staring at him blankly, and he cradled her shoulders and head to keep her off the ground.

After a few seconds of his hysterical prompting, Evelyn came around. She panicked when she didn't immediately recognize his face, but she soon regained her wits and calmed down. She clumsily stood up, and he helped balance her as she gained her footing.

"Are you okay?" he asked, guiding her to a nearby bench to sit down. The crowd had begun to disperse.

She stared at him, still mildly confused. "What happened?" Evelyn asked, trying to piece everything together.

"I have no idea." Will put his arm around her. "You just kinda spaced out and collapsed."

"Did I faint?" Evelyn asked, concerned that she'd made a scene.

"Not exactly. I mean, your eyes were open the whole time, but it was like your body. . . shut down?"

"What? I'm sorry. That's so embarrassing."

Will hugged her close. "Never apologize," he said. "I was just scared. I'm glad you're okay now."

She hugged him back. "Can we go home?"

"Let's go." He helped Evelyn to her feet and into a cab so he could accompany her home.

Will guided Evelyn upstairs to her apartment and to her bedroom. He placed a small glass of orange juice and a plate of saltine crackers on the nightstand in case she became faint again, then he tucked her in.

"You good?" he asked. "Need anything else?"

Evelyn smiled at him, deeply touched by his care. "You're not leaving, are you?"

"I don't have to. I mean, I can stay if you want me to."

"I want you to." She rolled over and flipped the comforter down on the empty side of the bed. "I need you to."

Without a word, Will kicked off his shoes and climbed into bed with her. He embraced her from behind, pulling her close, and they lay for a while, Evelyn taking in the warmth of his body and the rise and fall of his chest against her back. She thought he had gone to sleep, but soon there was a soft kiss on her left shoulder, and Will whispered in her ear, "I'm falling in love with you."

She smiled and pulled his arms tighter around her, wanting so badly to say it back, but something stopped her. She knew exactly what it was. She had to tell him her secret. Somehow she'd kept the dreamers' fate from him this long, but their relationship was getting serious fast, and she didn't want to hurt him. She squirmed away, sitting up to face him.

"Too soon. I'm sorry!" he said, sitting up to do damage control.

"No! No, it's not too soon!" Evelyn assured him. "It's just—" She wasn't sure how to articulate her thoughts and didn't want this to be the thing that drove him away. "I have to tell you something."

She talked for ten minutes, explaining everything she'd learned with Thomas and Dr. Holstead. Will sat with his head in his hands, trying to process what Evelyn had just told him. He inhaled deeply, held his breath for a few seconds, and exhaled until his lungs were empty. He straightened up, unsure of what to say.

"I know it's a lot. I'm sorry I didn't tell you sooner. I—" She paused to carefully choose her words. "I'm falling in love with you, too, and I didn't want you to run away." Evelyn held her breath, nervous.

He was silent for a long time before he finally spoke. "How do we stop it?" he asked, finally meeting her eyes for the first time.

"Stop what?" Evelyn replied, confused.

"How do we stop you, a dreamer, from dying like the others?" He threw the covers off himself.

"Well, I don't know for sure that I will die." She twisted her hands as she spoke. "I mean, it could be the other life that ends."

"I dunno," Will said, skeptical. "You just collapsed *tonight*. What if that's part of it?"

Evelyn's heart skipped a beat, and she was suddenly nauseous. She hadn't thought to connect the two.

"Do you really think that could have been the beginning?"

"I'm not sure." Will ran his hand through his hair. "You did say you hadn't eaten all day, so maybe not."

"See?" Evelyn said, putting her hand on his to reassure him. "I'm okay."

"For now," Will said. "Please go to a doctor tomorrow. Just to be sure."

She took his other hand also, their eyes locked on each other. "I am not going anywhere, okay?" She paused. "I love you."

He let go of her hands and entwined his fingers in her hair, pulling her face close for a passionate kiss that sent shockwaves through her whole body. In that moment, she forgot about the dreamers and everything else except Will, losing herself in his touch.

Chapter 27

1919

Back in Holstead's sitting room, Evelyn and Thomas thanked Ms. Brooks when she brought in a tray of finger sandwiches and poured them both hot tea.

"For you to nibble on while you wait for the doctor. Can I get you anything else?"

"No, thank you. These look lovely," Thomas said, reaching for a cucumber sandwich. Ms. Brooks left the room while Thomas and Evelyn quietly enjoyed the snack and waited for Holstead.

When the sitting room doors opened, they stood to greet Dr. Holstead as he shuffled in with his cane. "Sorry for the wait. I'm not as spry as I used to be."

"Not at all, Doctor." Evelyn smiled, sitting back down. "Thank you for meeting with us again."

Holstead startled at the sight of Thomas's bruised and swollen eye from his tousle with Calvin. "Well, you've been busy," Holstead said. "How did the other guy fare?"

Thomas chuckled at the idea. "I'm not much of a fighter, I'm afraid."

Holstead glanced back and forth between Evelyn and Thomas, piecing together their relationship.

"I see."

They detected a hint of amusement in his voice.

Dr. Holstead shifted his gaze to Evelyn as she sipped her tea, studying her. "Forgive me, my dear, but I am a bit confused. Are you studying the psychology of dreams along with Mr. Allen?"

Evelyn replaced her cup and saucer. "No," she said. "I am just . . . accompanying him. I think his studies are fascinating." She smiled sheepishly as she continued her lie. "You understand, I'm sure. Women don't get much opportunity to learn things like this, and I find myself insatiably curious."

"Well, who am I to stand in the way of women's empowerment? Shall we retreat to my study? I have some old notes there."

Evelyn and Thomas followed Dr. Holstead, leaving Ms. Brooks to clean up the tea. Soon, they were seated in Holstead's study, a dimly lit room lined with full bookshelves that held academic tomes and stacks of papers strewn around haphazardly.

"Sorry about the mess. I don't usually have anyone else in here. Not even Ms. Brooks."

"You don't have to tell me," Thomas joked. "A doctor's office is incomplete without a bit of a mess, don't you think?"

"Yes," Holstead agreed, shuffling through some books on the shelf. "Though I suppose it wouldn't do any harm for me to do a little filing sometime." A stack of papers fell as he removed a file folder from the shelf. He shrugged and waved them off.

Holstead made his way to his desk chair and sat down, untying the string that held the file folder closed.

"I hope my research notes will be of some help to you, Mr. Allen." Holstead pulled the contents of the folder out onto his desk. "Though I fear you may find them rather dull."

"I'd love to see anything you have about what happened to the dreamers before they died," Thomas said, leaning forward to get a closer view of the files. "I'm curious to learn more about how the dreams led to their physical demise."

"I can expand on that. Let me find the notes." As Holstead shuffled through the papers, Evelyn had a sudden urge to tell him the truth about herself. She tried to catch Thomas's eye for approval, but he was busy craning his neck to get a glimpse of the documents on the desk.

Evelyn took a deep breath, hoping what she was about to say wouldn't change the way Holstead thought of her. She didn't want to be a test subject. After a long, awkward silence, she finally spoke up.

"I'm a dreamer."

Holstead's jaw dropped, and his hands froze. After a few seconds, he grabbed a pen from his desk and flipped over a piece of paper from the stack in front of him. Evelyn watched him nervously. He leaned forward, placing his glasses on his nose.

"Tell me *everything*."

Evelyn spent the next half hour telling Holstead all about her dreams and some general information about her other life in 2003. Fascinated, Holstead jotted down notes while she talked. When she paused to catch her breath, Holstead put down his pen and sat back in his chair.

"Ms. Moore, can you tell me if you've noticed any . . . similarities," Holstead asked, "between your dream life and your real life as of late? Anything in your dreams that you've also noticed in your actual life?"

Evelyn thought for a moment before answering. She had been afraid of this question and more afraid of its answer. "Well, yes, a few things, I suppose."

"Can you tell me about them?"

Evelyn adjusted in her seat, unsure where Holstead was going with this line of questioning but anxious to find out. "Well," she said, "there was one thing that happened in both my dreams and my real life recently that was . . . notable, I suppose."

Holstead leaned forward and picked up his pen, raising his eyebrows at her.

"I was held at gunpoint. At a party—there. And in an alley—here."

Holstead scribbled something down. "Anything else?"

Taken aback that his first reaction hadn't been to express his condolences at her bad luck, Evelyn brushed it off and considered her answer to his question. "Yes!" she said, remembering. "In both places, I've been in romantic relationships with controlling, jealous men who have treated me poorly."

Thomas glanced at her, his eyes wide. He hadn't asked her much about her dreams, considering it improper, and besides, he wasn't sure if she wanted him—or anyone—to know. He didn't realize her dreams had been as difficult for her as her real life and found himself oddly protective of her.

"My 2003 boyfriend—*ex*-boyfriend, Cole—became upset when I got a ride home with Will—" As Evelyn said Will's name, the realization hit her like a ton of bricks. She'd been assaulted in both timelines because a man she wasn't dating accompanied her home and her abusive boyfriend caught them. She'd also never mentioned Will to Thomas.

"Evelyn, what is it?" Thomas asked, putting his hand on her forearm.

"Sorry," she said, shaking her head as if to dust off her thoughts. "I just realized something. Cole attacked me after I came home from coffee with my friend Will," she said. "He was jealous." Evelyn trailed off, but Thomas caught her train of thought.

"And Calvin attacked you here in 1919 after I dropped you off at your building." He sighed deeply.

The wheels in Thomas's head spun. Evelyn feared he would eventually realize she had a relationship with Will in 2003, and she hoped it wouldn't make him want to take a step back from her. Holstead interrupted both their musings.

"Would you say, Ms. Moore, that the similarities have been more frequent recently than they had been before?"

Evelyn considered it. "Yes, I would say so. I can't remember things happening at the same time like this before."

Holstead put down his pen and took off his glasses, placing them on the desk on top of the notes he'd just taken. He sighed heavily. Evelyn was worried she'd said the wrong thing.

"Ms. Moore, I'm afraid that what I'm about to tell you may be unsettling." His voice was suddenly laden with concern.

"What is it?" Evelyn asked. Her hands began to tremble, and Thomas placed his hand reassuringly upon hers.

"Two things I found in my studies with the dreamers," Holstead said thoughtfully, "are that they all had the same symptoms before they passed away." He paused, weighing his words. "And their dreams mirrored their real lives more and more leading up to their deaths."

Evelyn's mouth went dry, and she grabbed the edge of the desk to steady herself, gulping as she tried to focus on catching her breath.

Thomas stood and moved closer to her, putting a hand on her shoulder. "Evelyn, it's all right."

"I'm sorry, dear," Holstead said, slowly making his way around the desk to assist. "I didn't mean to frighten you. Bedside manner was never my strong suit." He put a finger below her right ear to take her pulse. "Well, you're still with us, anyway."

"How long did it take?" she asked, her face pale.

He hesitated, not wanting to deliver the news. "Weeks, sometimes a few months. Never more than a few months."

Evelyn doubled over in her chair, her face in her hands, realizing her fateful ending may have already begun. She hadn't told Thomas about collapsing in 2003 yet, and she didn't know exactly what it meant. She knew if she told him now, he would worry. She also knew if she didn't mention it, she'd lose her only chance at having someone who could actually help her stop it. She wasn't going to let Dr. Holstead get away. She needed him.

"It's already started," she whispered shakily into her hands. "I think it's already happening."

"What do you mean it's already happening?" Thomas asked, his voice loud with concern.

Evelyn told them about the incident outside the dining hall with Will in her dreams, leaving out the part where Will had professed his love for her and spent the night in her bed.

The lines on Thomas's forehead wrinkled as he processed all the new information. "I don't want to lose you, Evelyn."

She didn't want to lose him, either, and the idea that she may only have weeks with him was too much to bear. Desperate, Evelyn looked at Holstead. "Doctor, you have to help us," she pleaded, her eyes brimming with tears. "We have to find out how to stop it!"

"I—I don't—" Holstead sighed. "I'll see what I can do," he said finally. "In any case, we know that the dreamers who passed away in their other timelines lived on here. Presumably it works the opposite way, as well. If your fainting spells continue happening in 2003, chances are good you'll remain perfectly healthy in this life."

As he spoke, Evelyn remembered Caroline Huber. She couldn't believe she'd forgotten to mention Caroline to Holstead and Thomas before. She'd been so distracted with the news that she might already be dying. Caroline could very well be the key to finding the answers they needed. "I know what happened to Caroline Huber."

"What do you mean?" Holstead asked, his forehead crinkled. "Caroline Huber died in the late 1890s."

"Yes, she did." Evelyn paused to let the doctor catch on. "But she definitely lived on in her other timeline. In the 1960s. She was an activist and then became a choir director at a church upstate!"

Holstead was utterly confused. "How could you possibly know that?" he asked.

"I researched her in my college library in 2003." Evelyn said. "She's still alive!"

"Well, I never . . ." Holstead trailed off as he rubbed his chin, thinking over the vital information he'd just uncovered. "I always wondered what happened to Caroline in the other life."

"What does this mean for us?" Thomas caught himself. "For Evelyn, I mean."

Holstead calmed himself and got back to reality. "Forgive me. It means there's a good chance the two of you won't be separated anytime soon." Thomas and Evelyn stared at him intently. He went on. "We've never been able to confirm the longevity of a dreamer's life once they left this timeline. We now know Caroline lived a long time after she left this timeline, which bodes well for Evelyn. Especially if Evelyn's symptoms in 2003 match up with Caroline's in the 1890s. We don't know yet if her episode in 2003 had anything to do with the dreams, but even if it did, there's still hope for her here."

The blood drained from Evelyn's face again. She knew it was supposed to be good news, but at the same time it meant she could lose everything in 2003. Cammie, her parents, her activism. Will. She suddenly realized Thomas was speaking to her, interrupting her thoughts.

"Evelyn, did you hear the doc?"

Forcing a smile, she nodded. "That is a relief," she said, mustering all the happiness she could. She was going to live, but she was also going to die. She was fated to lose half of everything she'd ever known, and she had no way of knowing yet which life would end and which one would carry on. On the verge of tears, Evelyn stood up.

"I think I need to go home and lie down," she said. "This has all been a lot of shocking information for one night."

"Of course," Thomas said, standing to join her. "Let's get you back."

"Doctor, thank you," Evelyn said. "You have been more helpful than you know."

"Think nothing of it, dear." Holstead patted her back in a grandfatherly way. "I am sorry the news isn't all good."

"Good evening, Dr. Holstead." Thomas placed his hat on his head. "And thank you, truly."

"I'll forgive you for coming here under the guise of doctoral research, I suppose, Mr. Allen," said Holstead, winking at Evelyn.

"Apologies." Thomas smiled. "I hope you understand why we kept it quiet."

The doctor nodded, needing no further explanation.

"Good night, Doctor." Evelyn squeezed Holstead's hand warmly, making the old man smile. "Have a wonderful evening."

Thomas and Evelyn left Holstead's house and walked halfway down the block before either said a word.

"Well. That was . . . interesting," she said, breaking the silence.

He scoffed. "To put it lightly."

After walking in silence for a while, Evelyn sensed something was wrong. "What is it?"

"It's nothing."

"No, what is it?" she pressed.

"All right. I suppose I feel a little ridiculous because, if your timelines are mirroring each other, your friend Will is probably more than just a friend." His face turned red with embarrassment.

Evelyn linked her arm in his, pulling him close to her as they walked. She'd known this moment would come and was ready for it. "You're right," she said. "I do have a relationship with Will in 2003. But that doesn't have anything to do with you and me."

"It's just hard to make sense of everything when I'm pretty much jealous of a ghost," he said. "This is all so complicated. I can't say I've ever prepared myself for a situation quite like this."

Evelyn laughed. "I doubt anyone has." She paused to find the right words. "If I end up here for good, I want you to know I'll be yours. All yours."

A weak smile curled across his lips. "I hope that's true."

"I'm sorry this is happening," Evelyn said, her voice lowering. "I know it's complicated and unusual, and I never meant to get you caught up in any of it."

"I'm glad you did," he said, walking arm in arm with her. "I'll take you in real life or a dream any day for as long as I can get you."

"You say that now," she joked.

They walked back to her apartment, trying to forget all the heavy news they'd learned and focusing just on each other. She was strangely comforted knowing that she wouldn't lose everything all at once when she died. Most people didn't get that chance. Still, Evelyn hoped losing her dreams wouldn't hurt too much in her real life. She really did want to lean into this new relationship with Thomas. He was so perfect for her. But so was Will. A thousand emotions swirling in her head, Evelyn sat down to journal her thoughts. She didn't have the energy to write all the new things she'd learned about the dreamers, but she wouldn't be able to sleep if she didn't at least get out some of her thoughts about Thomas and Will.

Thomas just walked me home, and I notice each time we part, I am sadder to see him go. Things are moving at a slower pace than with Will in my other life, but the spark is turning more into a flame every minute I spend with Thomas.

Until recently I thought one of my lives was a dream, but the guilt is still eating at me. Will and Thomas are both such wonderful, giving men, and neither deserves to have to share me with someone else. Let alone someone else they could never hope to meet.

I never meant for it to happen, but I think I am in love with two men, and they live 84 years apart. It sounds absolutely mad, and I have no idea what I'll do about it.

The only place I can say this is here, but I think if Will and Thomas were in the same time and place, and I had to choose, I'd choose Will. There's an undeniable fire between us. The butterflies he gives me and his understanding—I never thought I'd find those. He's everything I ever wanted. It's natural.

Thomas is sweet, caring, and passionate in his own quiet way. I know he loves me, and each day I grow to care for him more. I can envision us being very happy together as well. I think there is something special between us. It's just going to take a bit longer for it to heat up.

Both men are fighting to keep me in their lives, and I would be lucky to end up with either of them.

I cannot say where my future with either of them will take me, but Thomas was right about one thing: this is going to be complicated and emotional. And no matter what happens, there will be unbearable heartache.

I hope I'm ready.

Chapter 28
2003

Evelyn woke up next to Will, and it was the best way she'd come out of a dream in years. He lay in her bed shirtless, propped up on a pillow and playing a game on his phone. She couldn't help but smile from ear to ear. It was like they'd been this way forever. She was so entranced by him that she forgot she'd had a fainting episode the night before.

She stretched, and Will flipped his phone shut. He smiled and rolled over to kiss her good morning. "Hey, sleepyhead. How are you feeling?"

Suddenly remembering her blackout spell outside the dining hall, Evelyn sat up to assess her body after a night's sleep. "I think I'm okay?" she said. "My head hurts a little, I guess."

"Want me to get you anything?" He caressed her upper arm with his fingertips as he lay on his side.

"I'm gonna take a shower," Evelyn said, kissing him before getting out of bed to find clothes for the day. "Maybe it'll refresh me and get my head back on straight."

"Sounds like a plan," Will answered, reopening his phone and sitting up in bed to resume his game. "I'm gonna make some coffee. You want tea?"

"I love that you always remember how much I hate coffee," she quipped.

"Ooooh, hate is such a strong word!" Will dramatically pretended to pierce his heart with a knife. "Who actually *hates* coffee?"

"Oh, we're just getting started," she retorted, climbing over the bed to kiss him again before she got into the shower. "There's so much more fun stuff you still have to learn about me!"

"You mean there's *more* than time traveling and hating coffee?"

"You have no idea," Evelyn said slyly, ducking into the bathroom and leaving Will chuckling to himself.

He watched the door close and waited for the sound of the shower turning on. When he was satisfied Evelyn was occupied, Will slid out of bed and went to her backpack. He rifled around until he found the printout from the library. He called the number for Caroline Huber's church and went into the living room while he waited for someone to answer.

After several rings, Will was about to hang up when he heard the click of someone picking up the phone. A man's voice was on the other end. "St. James, Angelo speaking. Can I help you?"

Will glanced at the bathroom door to make sure Evelyn was still in the shower before he spoke. "Yes, good morning. I recently moved to the area, and I'm hoping to find a new church to join," he lied. "I'm looking for a good choir, and I was told St. James had a wonderful choir director, a Caroline Huber?"

"Ah, yes!" Angelo said. "Caroline was a wonderful choir director for many years, but sadly her health forced her to step down a while back. We have a fantastic new director now, a real talent!"

Will hesitated, wondering how he could subtly find out if Caroline still attended the church even if she couldn't lead the choir. "How sad that Ms. Huber had to retire. I'm sure the new director is great."

"We're lucky Caroline still attends Mass every Sunday," Angelo said. "She wouldn't miss it!" He paused, waiting for a response, but Will was silent as he contemplated his next move.

"And you have Mass tomorrow morning?" Will asked, his idea coming together.

"We do!" cried Angelo, happy to be recruiting a new parishioner. "At ten o'clock. You're welcome to come and visit. See if it's a fit. We'd love to have you."

"I'll try, thank you!" said Will, hanging up the phone before Angelo could respond. Will pocketed his phone and went into the kitchen to get the coffee and tea started. When Evelyn eventually emerged from the bathroom, her hair in a towel and a fluffy yellow robe wrapped around her body, Will handed her a mug of hot tea.

"I gotta be honest, I don't know if I've ever actually made tea before, so I did my best." He laughed. "Feel free to chuck it out and start over if it's gross."

Evelyn sipped her tea, swallowing thoughtfully. "It's perfect." She smiled. "Thank you."

Will walked to the side of the island where Evelyn was sitting on a bar stool and sat next to her. "So, I have a confession to make. Don't be mad."

Immediately Evelyn braced for bad news. She didn't say anything, staring at him until he continued.

"I made a phone call while you were in the shower."

Scrunching her face in confusion, Evelyn waited for him to go on.

"I called Caroline's church in Saugerties. She doesn't direct the choir anymore, but she still goes every Sunday, and she's gonna be there tomorrow morning!"

Evelyn sipped her tea slowly, planning her answer. Her instinct was to be annoyed that Will had taken the issue into his own hands and called the church without consulting her first, but at the same time, Evelyn knew he was freaked out at the prospect of losing her, and he was compelled to help. "Okay, so you're saying we should, what? Go to church tomorrow morning?"

"I mean, if we want to talk to Caroline, yeah. I think we should. What if she has the information we need to keep you safe?"

"I understand. But is it really okay to ambush an old lady at church on a Sunday and ask her about things that might be traumatic for her?"

"Well, when you put it like that it sounds bad," Will replied. "I just want to figure this out. Quickly."

She sensed the desperation in his voice. She put down her tea and stood up, positioning her body between his knees. "I get it." She hugged him. "You're right. Let's go to church."

Exhaling with relief, Will hugged her back tightly, the towel wrapped around her wet hair making it hard for him to find a comfortable place to put his face. "I'm clueless about church. I have no idea what to do when I'm there. My parents never really took me," he said as he pulled away.

"I'm not much help." Evelyn giggled. "I don't think I've been since I was five!"

"We'll figure it out," Will said, his facing turning serious. "We'll figure it all out."

"I know we will," Evelyn said, hugging him again.

Before sunrise the next morning, they piled into his car and headed upstate. Evelyn wrung her hands as they drove. What if Caroline had no information at all? What if she did, and it was bad news? She took in the scenery as they drove up the highway, wishing she'd never found out any information about the dreamers. In a way, she had been better off not knowing what happened to them. At least then she didn't have to spend every waking moment worried she was going to lose so much, and that it could happen at any time. She looked over at Will and grinned to herself. He caught her staring at him.

"What?" he said, smiling at her.

"Nothing. You just make me happy."

"Same." He reached over to take her hand.

They drove in silence until they finally reached the quaint little church building where they hoped to find Caroline. Will selected a parking spot away from the entrance, and they waited as the lot slowly filled with cars arriving for the service. When there were about five minutes left until the church bells rang, they exited the car and made their way inside.

They chose a seat in the back of the church. Evelyn admired the beautiful stained glass windows as the morning sun shone through them and cast a warm glow over the room. A dull chatter echoed through the building as the weekly parishioners caught up with each other ahead of Mass. Evelyn and Will had been greeted by some of them when they'd sat, but no one had made conversation yet, to Evelyn's relief.

Soon, Mass began. The priest, a red-faced, jovial old man with a tuft of white hair on his head that almost made him resemble a mad scientist, greeted the congregation and welcomed newcomers to the church.

Evelyn leaned over and whispered in Will's ear, "I hope he doesn't ask new people to stand and introduce themselves."

"If you are here for the first time, won't you please stand so we can welcome you to St. James," the priest said, beaming. Evelyn and Will looked at each other and tried not to laugh, amused at their luck. The people sitting near them stared at them, knowing they weren't familiar faces. The two stood, smiling awkwardly as the priest welcomed them. To their relief, he allowed them to sit back down without having to say anything in front of everyone.

Mass was nice but unremarkable, as far as Evelyn and Will could tell. They weren't exactly experts, but they made a good show of it by attempting to sing the hymns and joining in the various prayers and the call and response. Evelyn actually liked some of the songs. They brought a sense of calm over her, which she welcomed in the midst of so much uncertainty. At one point, there was communion. Evelyn and Will weren't sure if they should participate or exactly how it worked.

"Do you think it's juice or wine?" she whispered.

"There are kids doing it, so I guess juice?"

She nodded as she sat, scanning the line of people, trying to guess which one of them was Caroline.

As the service wrapped up, they followed the parishioners to a small tent on the lawn with tables of doughnuts and coffee. The priest had invited everyone to come, and Evelyn and Will thought perhaps it was the best way to meet Caroline.

At the coffee bar, someone grabbed Evelyn's arm from behind, startling her. She whirled around to face an old woman whose gray shoulder-length hair was unkempt, but her dark eyes were piercing. Evelyn waited for the woman to say something, sure she was about to be recruited for a church knitting group.

"You have the dreams!" the old woman whispered, tightening her grip on Evelyn's arm.

Evelyn's body went cold at the woman's words.

"Are you Caroline?" Will said, alarmed at the sudden exchange.

"Yes." She didn't let go of Evelyn. "You're like me. You have the dreams. Where do you go?"

Confused, Evelyn shook her head. "I'm sorry, where do I go? For what?"

"In your dreams! Where do you go when you dream?"

Evelyn's mouth was suddenly dry. The plan to go to the church and meet Caroline had been so rushed she hadn't taken the time to prepare herself for being in the presence of the only person she'd ever met who understood everything she was going through. "I—I go to the early 1900s," she whispered, knowing how odd the conversation would sound to anyone else. "Actually, 1919, right now."

"I knew it! I was there!" Caroline's eyes were wide.

"You were . . . where?" Evelyn asked. "You were in 1919?"

"Not exactly. I died before that!" Caroline laughed, confusing Evelyn and Will. "But I was there before. When the doctors did the experiments."

Evelyn and Will glanced at each other. "Experiments?" Will asked. "Do you mean Dr. Fletcher and Dr. Holstead?"

"They wanted to know all about my dreams!" Caroline said, waving her hands in front of her as if to conjure up something. She laughed again. "All that work, and they still don't know how it ended! And I can't tell them! Because I'm here!"

Evelyn and Will realized Caroline Huber wasn't exactly in her right mind. The trip might not be as fruitful as they hoped, but they wouldn't let the opportunity go to waste. Will kindly pressed Caroline for more information.

"Ms. Huber, do you remember what happened to you before you died? In the—in your—uh—"

"In your dream life," Evelyn interrupted, saving Will from himself. "Do you remember anything about the months or weeks before you . . . passed? Back then?"

Caroline's expression changed from amused to serious. "It all came together," she said, her voice lowering. "It was all the same! And then the blackouts started." She clenched her jaw and took a sharp breath as she reminisced, but Evelyn and Will didn't want to cause a scene.

"We don't have to talk about it if you don't want to, Caroline," Evelyn said. "I'm sorry if we upset you."

All the clarity in the world suddenly shone through Caroline's dark brown irises. "Once it starts, you don't have much time. Everything will be the same. In your dreams, your real life. The blackouts will get worse. That's how you'll know." Caroline's voice was getting louder as she spoke, her tone conveying urgency and desperation. She grabbed Evelyn's arm again. "Don't ever let them tell you you're crazy! You're not crazy! *I'm* not crazy! We're special!"

Many of the things Caroline said didn't make sense, but Evelyn knew there were some answers within those words.

"How did you know she was a dreamer?" Will asked, gesturing to Evelyn.

It was strange that Caroline had recognized her as a fellow dreamer. Evelyn had no memory of ever meeting her before in either timeline.

Before Caroline could answer, a young woman walked over, putting her arm around the old woman's shoulders to calm her down. "Hey, Caroline!" The young woman smiled. "You okay?"

Caroline glared at Evelyn and Will. They all knew they couldn't continue the conversation with anyone else around.

"I'm sorry, we didn't mean to upset her," Will said politely. "We're new here, and we're just trying to meet a few people from the church."

"She'll be all right," the woman said cheerfully.

"I'll be fine," Caroline echoed. The way she stared at Evelyn, Evelyn could tell she had more she wanted to say.

"Let's go get you a cup of coffee," the young woman said, nodding goodbye to Will and Evelyn as she guided Caroline over to the coffee bar.

When they'd moved a few feet away, Caroline turned back toward Evelyn and Will and shouted, "You can't get away from the dreams, even after they're gone! You'll see!"

Caroline's companion rubbed her upper arm as she turned the woman around and headed her toward the coffee bar.

Evelyn's feet were rooted to the ground.

"Let's get out of here," Will said, snapping her out of her thoughts. They ditched their plates in a nearby garbage can.

Once they were in the car and buckled in, Evelyn sat back in the passenger seat and let out a deep sigh. "What *was* that, Will?"

"I don't know." He started the car. "It's hard to say which pieces of what Caroline told us are true and which are a result of her not remembering things clearly."

"How did she know I was a dreamer?" Evelyn wondered aloud. "I've never met her. At least I don't think I have."

"I'm not sure." Will pulled out of the parking lot. "But we did find out one thing. You can definitely live on for decades in one of your timelines."

"Yes, meeting her in the flesh confirms that one life carries on normally, right?" Evelyn said, glad they seemed to have solved at least one part of the mystery. She was still leery about the whole thing. "What she said was a little scary, wasn't it? What did she mean when she said I'll never escape the dreams? I'm so confused."

"I'm not sure. That was definitely weird," he said thoughtfully. "I think the most important thing we know now is that as soon as the blackouts start—*if* they start—we don't have much time to figure out how to stop you from losing this timeline."

"I don't know if we *can* stop it," she said, closing her eyes and leaning her head on the headrest. She thought for a few seconds before she continued. "Maybe it's just something that has to happen. Maybe it would be best if I let you go now. Before things get any harder for you."

The car lurched as Will hit the brakes and swerved onto the shoulder. He twisted in his seat to face her, his jaw set. He grabbed both of her shoulders, turning her so she faced him.

"Listen to me," he said, his voice serious. "I am going to fight for you, Evelyn. And I'm not gonna let this ruin what we have. I don't care if we have a few weeks or a few months or the rest of our lives. I want to spend as much time with you as I can."

A loud sob burst out of Evelyn before she could stop it.

Unbuckling his seatbelt to hug her, Will tried to comfort her. "It's gonna be okay," he whispered.

Evelyn dabbed the tears from under her eyes. "It's not okay, Will," she said. She paused for a few seconds, drying her hands on her pants. "But if it's not okay, I'd rather it not be okay with you here."

"And I am here. I'm not going anywhere, I promise." He waited a few seconds, holding her as he contemplated what to say next. "Nothing has happened yet that we know of for certain. We don't know how long we have. It could be years, still. It might not happen in this timeline at all."

"Will, I almost fainted the other night outside the dining hall!" she said as she pulled away. "What if it's *already* started?"

Will sat back in his seat, covering his face with his hands. He took some time to formulate the exact words to say to her before turning and taking her hands in his. Her palms were still damp with tears.

"Then let's just enjoy our time," he said quietly. "Let's not spend it chasing after theories and loopholes. Unless you want to."

Evelyn gazed at him. She knew he would be with her no matter what, and no matter how long, but she wasn't willing to let the dreams tear him away so easily. "No," she said firmly. "We can do both."

"What do you mean?" he asked.

"We're going to enjoy our time, *and* I'm going to keep working on how to stay here. With you," she said resolutely. "I'm gonna figure it out."

"We'll do whatever you want to do," Will said, taking her face softly in his hand. "I'm here. No matter what. Okay?"

"Okay." She took his hand in her own, pressing her forehead against his, more tears rolling down her cheeks. "I love you."

"I love you, too."

They sat that way for a while on the side of the road, her face in his palm, as they tried to make sense of their extraordinary situation. Evelyn knew deep down she couldn't stop the progression of things if they had already begun, and she promised herself she wouldn't take a second with Will for granted.

They drove back to the city, hand in hand as the sky darkened and rain began to fall. They sat in silence most of the way, knowing nothing they said would take away the weight of what they'd learned that day. Evelyn closed her eyes, almost drifting off before jolting herself awake as she realized every moment she slept was one moment less she could spend with Will. She turned on the radio, quickly finding a song they both liked. They made small talk and joked as they finished their drive home, trying to savor every laugh they shared as if it were their last. For all Evelyn knew, it might be.

Chapter 29
1919

Evelyn had become very conscious lately of how quickly time passed, no matter which life she was living. More than ever, she had learned to appreciate the importance of every moment with the people she loved.

She hurried to the office early to meet Thomas for breakfast before work. It had become one of their favorite things to do together, and she loved starting her days with him.

He was waiting near the doors when she turned the corner. She smiled at him and picked up her pace. As she approached, he walked to meet her, a welcoming grin on his face.

"Good morning," he said, taking her hand in his and kissing it lightly. He didn't let go.

"Good morning, Thomas. It really is nice to start my workday like this."

"Can I buy you a tea?" he asked.

She was touched that, just like Will, he remembered she didn't like coffee. Evelyn linked arms with him, heading toward the coffee shop. His arm warmed her body in the cold. Since it wasn't socially acceptable to get closer to him, Evelyn savored what heat she could. He opened the door, ushering her inside. The warmth of the shop and smell of fresh doughnuts thawed Evelyn immediately as the two sat at a small booth near the window.

Evelyn knew she had to tell him about meeting Caroline and what she'd learned about the dreams. As the waitress poured hot coffee for Thomas, he ordered hot tea for Evelyn. He made a point not to touch his coffee until Evelyn's tea arrived. Those little things made him such a compassionate gentleman. She couldn't keep the secret from him a moment longer.

"I met Caroline Huber," she blurted out.

Thomas's eyes widened. "You—you *met* Caroline Huber? The same Caroline who supposedly died two decades ago?"

"Yes." She paused. "Well, no. I mean—" She sighed, trying to gather her thoughts. "Let me start again. In my other life, I met the Caroline from Holstead and Fletcher's studies!"

Thomas sat back in his seat, dropping his arms loosely to his sides. He stayed silent a while, the wheels turning in his head as he figured out what Evelyn meeting 1960s Caroline meant. Eventually he spoke.

"So, what you're saying is that you found absolute proof that if you die in your other life, you'll live on here? With me? It doesn't shorten your life or complicate your health?"

"Well, yes. But if I go away in this timeline, I'll live on in the other one."

He took her hands across the table, his eyes wide with excitement. "So there's a good chance I'm not going to lose you?"

"A good chance," Evelyn repeated, moved by how happy he was at the news. "I mean, I'm still scared of losing either life. They've both been part of me for as long as I've been alive." She stared at their hands linked on the tabletop. "Do you promise *you* won't go anywhere if I stay?"

He tightened his grip on her hands and leaned forward, his face firm. "I'm not going anywhere."

She swallowed. Will had said the exact same words to her just hours before. She needed to work through so many things regarding the impending change, but she was comforted knowing Thomas would be there to help get her through losing her other life, if that's how it all went.

After a few moments of silence, Thomas let go of Evelyn's hands, sitting back in his seat as the waitress delivered the tea. Taking his first sip of coffee, Thomas asked Evelyn to tell him more about meeting Caroline Huber.

"Well, I wouldn't exactly say she's in her right mind, unfortunately," she began.

"Was she able to tell you anything that might help you stay in both your timelines?"

"Well, no, not exactly." Evelyn's voice lowered. "She just said once the blackouts start, there's nothing you can do to stop it."

"Well, that isn't the news I was hoping you'd find out." Thomas was genuinely sorry for Evelyn as she tangled with the complexities of imminently losing half her life. "Did she tell you anything else? Anything at all that might help us figure out how to save your dreams?"

"No. She told me I'd never escape the dreams, even if I lost them. But she never told me what she meant. I don't even know if *she* knows what she meant."

"Maybe she's still having the dreams? Or the dreams started again?"

"I don't know," Evelyn said. "Someone came and took her away, and I couldn't get any more information from her."

"Maybe you could go back? Ask her some more questions?"

"Maybe." Evelyn sipped her tea. "I don't know if Will would want to go to church again, though." She immediately regretted her words. Will's name just slipped out.

"Will went with you. I see." Thomas fixed his gaze on the table, deep in thought.

"What is it?" Evelyn asked, sure she already knew the answer.

"It's just hard for me to imagine you being with someone else. There. In the dreams. Your other life," he said flatly. "I guess I'm still feeling a bit jealous. Stupid, right?" He scoffed. "Jealous of a dream."

"You don't have to be jealous, Thomas." Evelyn reached over and took one of his hands again. "It's just dreams."

"It's just dreams?" He slid his hand out of her grip. "Evelyn, it's a whole other life. A real life. And if I'm understanding correctly, you have a whole other relationship there with Will?"

"Well, yes." Evelyn was unsure how to respond. "But that doesn't matter here with you."

"Of course it matters," he snapped, surprising Evelyn. She'd never heard that tone in his voice before. He took a deep breath and continued more calmly. "It matters because I'm falling in love with you, and I don't know how to share you with someone else."

Evelyn sat back in her seat, nervous that he put her on the spot. "I'm falling in love with you, too," she finally uttered.

He paused for a while. "And you love him as well?" His voice cracked slightly.

"Yes, Thomas! Okay? It doesn't matter anyway because I'm probably going to die there soon, and I'll never get to see him again!" A tear rolled down her cheek.

Thomas inhaled deeply. This was more than just a simple case of jealousy. He scolded himself for not being more sensitive to her situation and letting his emotions get the best of him. "I'm sorry you're facing this," he said quietly. "I'm sorry I don't know how to handle this situation. I'm sorry I don't know how not to be jealous of a person who isn't even real. All I know is I am falling in love with you, Evelyn, and I don't want to do that if your heart is with someone else. Even if it's in a dream or another lifetime."

"I can't help what my heart does in 2003," she said, her voice strained. "But I *can* tell you it doesn't mean I love you any less here."

He stared at her for a painfully long few seconds before speaking again. "Tell me one thing. Do you love him more than you love me?"

"*What?*" Evelyn was shocked he would dare ask. He was more than aware of everything she was dealing with. Why would he pile on with his jealousy, and how could he expect her to choose between two men she loved?

"It's a simple question, Evelyn."

"You're putting me in a no-win situation, Thomas! This isn't fair."

He stood, putting on his coat. "That's all the answer I need," he said, tossing a few coins on the table to cover their order before heading out of the store.

Evelyn swallowed the painful lump in her throat as she watched him leave. She had never meant to hurt him but had hoped he'd be more understanding about her unique set of circumstances. Still, it was a lot for anyone to handle, and she didn't fully blame him for walking out on her. She told herself she was lucky he'd stuck around this long with all the drama she brought with her. After one last sip of her tea and dabbing her eyes dry with a napkin, Evelyn left the coffee shop and headed toward her office. She'd probably just lost Thomas and hadn't been prepared for how much not having him in her life hurt. They'd become so close, and he was all she had in this timeline. She didn't want to go through losing 2003 without him. As she walked along the sidewalk dodging other pedestrians, she realized she didn't want to do anything in this life without him.

Chapter 30

2003

Will had kept his plans for their date that evening a closely guarded secret. All he'd told her was to dress up and not ask any questions. The car finally stopped, and Will took her hand as he assisted her onto the sidewalk.

"Where are we?" Evelyn was dying to know.

"Not yet," he said, paying the driver and sending the car on its way. "C'mon, almost there."

He led her along the sidewalk. A gust of wind hit her as Will knocked on the door of a spectacular house. Evelyn couldn't imagine how Will knew anyone who lived in a house like it.

"Okay, close your eyes," Will said.

"Wait, seriously?" His antics amused her.

"Trust me."

She dutifully closed her eyes, and Will took her hand. The door clicked open, and he guided her inside, where the aroma of cooking food filled her senses.

"Ready?" Will asked.

"So ready!" Evelyn gasped when she opened her eyes. A beautifully decorated table sat in the center of a gorgeous dining room. She was in awe of the lavish decor and luxurious furnishings.

"Where are we?" she asked. They were the only two people in the room. The opulent space boasted floor-to-ceiling windows on three sides and a grand city garden with the most perfect landscaping Evelyn had ever seen. A fountain in the middle of the yard was surrounded by pristine topiary and flower beds twinkling with lights. It was magical.

"It's incredible!"

"It's a famous old Manhattan party house that has since been sold and turned into a very upscale, very exclusive, *very* romantic private dining experience for celebrating special occasions." He smiled, proud he had managed to impress her. He'd promised a date where she would be totally safe from Cole and anything else, and he'd delivered beyond her wildest dreams.

"And what is tonight's special occasion?" she asked, a coy smile on her face.

"Us. You and me. For however long we have."

A white-gloved server entered the room carrying a bottle of champagne resting on his forearm. Will nodded his approval, and the server popped the cork and poured them each a glass. After he left, Will raised his arm in a toast. "To us."

She clinked her glass against his.

Evelyn turned around again, soaking up her surroundings. The setting was oddly familiar, but she couldn't recall if she'd ever come to a place like this. She'd been to a lot of galas and other engagements in the city for her political activism ever since her freshman year. It was impossible to remember them all.

"Stunned silent. Probably the best reaction I could have hoped for." He smirked.

"Sorry." She laughed. "This place is just . . . perfect. Thank you for bringing me here."

"You look beautiful tonight," Will said, gazing at her.

Embarrassed, Evelyn smiled and lowered her eyes. She had never been good at accepting compliments. Will sat across from her in a sharply pressed dinner jacket and button-down shirt, his dark hair as always a little unruly no matter what he did to tame it. "You look pretty amazing yourself."

He stood and walked around the table to Evelyn. "I thought maybe we could go outside for a minute," he said. He escorted her through the sliding glass door. As they approached the glittering fountain in the middle of the yard, soft music began to play. Evelyn cocked her head to figure out where it had come from. Will stopped walking and held out his hand. "May I have this dance?"

Evelyn couldn't help but giggle. The twinkling lights everywhere, the fountain, her long green satin gown, and Will were all simply perfect. She put one arm around his waist, and they held hands as they danced alone in the beautiful garden. The city noise grew faint, and in that moment she felt like they were the only two people in the world. She rested her head on his chest and drank in the smell of his cologne, the warmth of his arms around her, and the tenderness of his hand in hers. She pulled back to look up at him. "I can't believe this is real."

"You deserve it. You have no idea how special you are, Evelyn."

"No one has ever done anything like this for me," she said softly. "Thank you for showing me what love is. While I'm still here."

"I don't care what happens with the dreams." Will said, suddenly standing still. "I'm going to spend every moment we have, no matter how many there are, making sure you know how loved you are."

"How did I get lucky enough to find you?" she whispered. "Why couldn't it have been sooner?"

"We weren't ready," Will said, beginning their dance again. "The universe knew when it was the right time."

They danced in silence for a few more minutes before Will suggested they return to the table for dinner. They made their way back in, arm in arm. Will was right. Evelyn couldn't remember ever being so loved. Cole and the gunman at the party and everything else were distant memories, and she knew she had to savor every second she had with him.

They talked and laughed over every course of the decadent dinner Will had organized. When they were finished, they thanked the waiter and asked him to please give their compliments to the chef. Will draped Evelyn's coat over her shoulders before they entered the foyer to leave the beautiful Manhattan edifice. Evelyn paused to take in the grandness of it all one more time. For the first time since she arrived, she raised her eyes for any elaborate lighting or ceiling art or crown molding.

As soon as she caught sight of the chandelier, the room started spinning. Sounds became fuzzy, and she struggled to form the words to explain to Will what was happening. The last thing Evelyn remembered before she faded to black was the light fixture above. It was the rectangular crystal chandelier she had coveted when she'd left this very house in her dreams in 1919 after the party with Emily, Lily, and Ada. She'd danced and drank in that exact backyard near the fountain. And she'd admired the very same glittering chandelier eighty-four years in the past.

An hour later, Evelyn lay in a hospital bed, having finally regained her composure. Will was by her side when she opened her eyes after a brief nap, which didn't surprise her in the least, but she still felt guilty that she'd ruined their perfect night.

"I'm so sorry," she said for what seemed like the hundredth time since she came to. "I really wish this hadn't happened. I was having the best night of my life."

"Nope, we're not doing apologies for this!" Will adjusted her blankets and straightened her pillow. "I'm just glad you're okay. That was super scary, Evelyn."

"I know. I'm sorry."

He glanced at her, reminding her not to apologize.

"I mean, not *sorry*." She smiled. "But you know. That was probably terrifying, and I wish you hadn't been there to see it."

"I'm fine. I just want you to rest up so we can get you out of here and back home where you belong. So I can take care of you."

"Oh, I get my own hot private nurse?" she joked. "Well, this really is the best night ever!"

He laughed. "Hey, I almost forgot. I've got something for you." He reached into his jacket pocket. "So you'll never forget this night. Well, the good part of the night." He dropped something into her outstretched palm.

"The champagne cork!" Evelyn was deeply touched that he'd been so sentimental to keep the cork from the bottle they'd opened at dinner. And that he'd known she was the type of person who would do the exact same thing. Examining it more closely, she noticed some writing in blue ink. *The night of my dreams. —Will.*

"I'm keeping this forever." She held it close to her heart. "Thank you for tonight."

"You're welcome," he said. "But I think it's time to wrap it up, don't you? I'm gonna go find a nurse and speed this up. Wait here."

"I'll be right here," Evelyn said sarcastically. He scoffed at her joke, and she smiled. He really did get her.

Alone for the first time since she'd arrived at the hospital, Evelyn began to process what had happened that night. Her blood chilled upon realizing the fierce blackout more than likely meant the beginning of the end for her in this timeline. She had no way of knowing when the next blackout would happen, but she was more determined than ever to spend every minute she could with Will. She was exhausted, and the blackout had turned her brain to mush, but she knew if she slept, she would go back to 1919, where she'd be forever after she left this life, and she'd miss precious time with Will that she could never get back.

Evelyn secretly vowed to stay awake for as many hours as she could possibly stand. She straightened herself up when Will re-entered the room, a nurse trailing behind him with a stack of paperwork in her hands.

"Look, you're going home!" Will said happily.

While she filled out the discharge papers, Evelyn wondered how long a human could stay awake without breaking down. She didn't care. The exhaustion would be worth it. She'd have to talk to him at some point about what the blackout meant, but she wanted to salvage what she could of their night and so decided to wait until morning.

An hour later, the two arrived back at Evelyn's apartment. Will headed directly for her bedroom, where he turned down the blankets and fluffed the pillows. The sound of the living room television startled him out of the bedroom. Evelyn was sitting on the couch, wrapped in the throw blanket, flipping through the channels. She patted the couch next to her, inviting him to sit with her.

"I thought you'd want to sleep," Will said, not moving from the bedroom door.

"No, I think I'd rather sit with you and watch something. If you want to?"

Will knew he should encourage her to rest, but he also knew Evelyn Moore wouldn't be swayed, so he sat next to her.

"Ooh, *Simple Life* marathon!" Evelyn said, setting the remote on the couch.

"Whatever you like," Will said, amused that the same girl he'd met on campus protesting a multinational war was also into a show about celebrities knowing absolutely nothing about the world. Her quirks were his favorite part. He put his arm around her and snuggled her close to him. They sat like that for a while, laughing at Paris Hilton and Nicole Richie struggling to make sense of rural life.

A few times, Evelyn got drowsy, so she adjusted her position to keep herself awake. At one point, she asked Will to boil her some water for a cup of hot tea. She didn't tell him what she really wanted was caffeine. Sipping on her tea, Evelyn wondered how long she could stay awake on purpose without him catching on.

It was getting late, and she knew she couldn't keep *him* awake for days, but she resolved to stay up and savor his presence. She thought maybe she would do a few things on her bucket list, like write a poem or finally read *Gone with the Wind*. Maybe she could join one of those online Texas hold 'em sites everyone was raving about and win some money before her time was up. She could donate it to one of her causes and do some good with the days she had left. After a few minutes of such thoughts running through her mind,

Evelyn realized she was literally sitting around planning her last acts on earth, and the idea that she'd been so nonchalant about it so far scared her a bit.

Evelyn imagined her parents finding out she'd passed. Her grandparents. Her friends. Cammie would be devastated. Her throat tightened, and her eyes began welling up. Evelyn cut off her thoughts before she got to the part of Will mourning her. She would have plenty of time to deal with her emotions after he went to sleep. She needed every moment with him to be perfect right now, and she wasn't going to cloud it with her depressing, unavoidable fate.

"Come on, let's go to bed. You're exhausted," she said. "And at some point, I guess I should change out of this gown." She laughed, realizing she hadn't even put on pajamas when she got home.

"I'll go to bed, but I'm formally petitioning for the gown to stay." He smiled, heading to the bedroom.

"As you wish," Evelyn said, following him. She closed the door behind her and climbed into bed with him, still draped in the green dress she'd worn to their spectacular dinner earlier that evening. She snuggled up to Will, resting her head on his chest, his heart beating in her ear. He played with her hair as they lay in silence. She sensed he was hesitating to make a move on her, but the truth was, she didn't feel *that* bad, and the doctor had warned that the side effects from her episode might not set in until the next day.

She slid the covers down suggestively. He didn't need any other hint.

A while later, the rhythmic rise and fall of Will's chest under her head told her he was asleep. After waiting a few more minutes, she eventually lifted herself off him, sitting up in bed to admire him for a few seconds. She couldn't believe she had fallen for him so hard in such a short time. It was cruel, really, for life to give them this beautiful, perfect love and then threaten to rip it away so soon.

With her alone time, Evelyn decided she would write letters to everyone she loved, telling them how much they meant to her.

Hours later, she'd written a pile of letters that had made her emotions swirl and her memories run wild. All she had left were Cammie, Will, and her parents, and she couldn't bring herself to start writing to them. She needed a break.

Evelyn opened her laptop and began scouring photos of herself with her friends and family. The idea that this would soon be relegated to a collection of memories was almost too much to bear. Unplugging the computer, she carried it into the living room, quietly closing the bedroom door behind her, and sat on the couch. Scrolling through more photos, Evelyn couldn't help but sob.

Once she'd cried all her tears, she tiptoed into the bedroom and retrieved the notepad. Back in the living room, she breathed deeply before putting pen to paper to write some of the hardest words she'd ever written.

Dear Cammie,

My sweet, beautiful, amazing best friend. I am the luckiest girl in the world to have had you by my side my whole life, like a sister delivered to me by fate instead of family. Without you, I would have been lost. Especially after moving to New York. You've always been home to me, and I hope you know you've made everything here easier, more fun, and more normal for me.

Evelyn wrote out some of her favorite memories with Cammie before asking her friend the impossible.

Cam, I need you to look after Will when I'm gone. Please check on him and make sure he's okay. I'm worried about him. We've fallen hard and fast, and I don't know how else to explain it except that this has been the love of a lifetime, and he'll be devastated when it ends. You're the only one I trust to watch over him for me.

Evelyn put down her pen and decided to write more the next night. She was emotionally drained. She packed her letters away so Will wouldn't find them and turned on her laptop to look up the rules of Texas hold 'em.

Chapter 31
2003

Evelyn was still awake when Will opened his eyes the next morning. She'd come back to bed in time for him to wake up so he'd think she'd been there all night. She didn't want him to worry about her, but her hours were precious, and she didn't want to waste them sleeping.

Will smiled as he rolled over and saw her. He pulled himself closer to her and put his arm over her, hugging her. "How are you doing?"

"Okay," she replied, returning his hug and giving him a kiss. "Got a little headache, like the doctor said I would."

"Well, don't you worry about a thing," Will said, jumping out of bed and pulling his jeans on. "I'm gonna take care of you all day." Evelyn studied his every move as he put on a T-shirt and shoes.

"Where are you going?"

"Breakfast," he said, tying the laces on his sneakers. "Sausage or bacon?"

"Wait, don't you have class?"

"Yes, but I've never missed this class before, so I think I can get away with skipping once."

"Are you sure?"

"Bacon or sausage?"

"I wanna come with you," Evelyn said, sliding out of bed to grab some clothes.

"Shouldn't you stay here and rest?"

"I'm not wasting any time lying around in my apartment alone." She pulled her hair into a messy bun. "I want to go with you."

"No arguments from me!" he yelled as he entered the bathroom to brush his teeth.

Evelyn followed him and hugged him from behind. He smiled at her reflection in the mirror. She put her mouth close to his ear to whisper to him. He leaned in, curious what she had to say.

"Bacon."

They left the apartment and walked down the city street, Evelyn being mindful of every noise, every smell, and every quirk New York had to offer. She loved living here so much, and she was glad she would get to stay in the city in 1919, but it just wasn't the same. The modern city was so alive, abuzz with the energy of the thousands of people who came here from all over the world to achieve their dreams. Everyone was always in a hurry. The bustling sidewalks, the smell of the food from the street vendors, and the fumes from the cars and the subway gave the city a thriving pulse. The city in 1919 was vastly different, and though she loved it there as well, she would miss this undeniably energetic place as it was in this life.

A wave of exhaustion suddenly rolled over Evelyn. The blackout had really taken a toll, leaving her body drained. She wanted so badly to sleep without missing time with Will, but she knew to soak up time with him and do everything on her list, she had to stay awake. She told Will to wait outside while she ducked into the corner store to buy a lottery ticket. When she met him back outside, she was holding an energy drink. She handed him the ticket.

"Good luck!" She smiled. Will examined the ticket before pocketing it, and Evelyn chugged as much of the drink as she could. She hated energy drinks, but if it would keep her awake, she was willing to drink gallons of it.

"Thirsty?" Will asked, watching her gulp it down.

"Just figured I could use the jolt."

They eventually arrived at the deli and ordered breakfast sandwiches. Taking their food to go, Will turned to walk back to the apartment, but Evelyn grabbed his arm and urged him the other direction. "Breakfast in the park?"

"Sure," Will said as they began walking to Washington Square Park.

It was one of Evelyn's favorites. Its rich history connected her to the New York City of the past. Which made sense since she'd spent literally half her life there. She hoped being in this park with Will now would make it a place she could visit in 1919 to remember him and somehow be close to him. The park had been there since the 1800s and was one of the few places in the city that hadn't completely disappeared or been turned into a parking garage since the industrial boom of the early 1900s. She still hadn't talked to him about the fact that the blackout likely meant she was going to die in this life. She was waiting for the right moment, but when was the right time to discuss that kind of news?

They found a bench and sat down to eat and people-watch. They played a game where they created a name and occupation for each passerby based solely on appearance. They were laughing uncontrollably after a while of outlandish job titles and pun-filled fake names. Evelyn wished the morning would never end. She was physically exhausted, but it was worth it. Will was worth it.

She spent the rest of the day with him, walking the city, watching movies on her couch, and just enjoying his company. She was so taken with him she forgot about her depressing fate a few times throughout the day.

Around eleven o'clock that night, Will told her he was getting tired. She agreed and went through her bedtime routine as normal, changing into a matching pajama set and washing her face. Finally in bed with him, she wrapped herself in his arms and nuzzled in close.

"Your feet are freezing." He smirked, rubbing his warm feet on hers to help heat them up.

"Who needs socks when I've got you?" she said, giggling as his feet tickled her own. Soon, Will fell asleep with her head on his chest again. Evelyn lay there a long time, willing herself to stay awake in spite of his rhythmic breathing threatening to lull her to sleep. When he shifted positions, she carefully lifted herself off him and slipped out of bed as she had the night before.

Evelyn padded into the kitchen and turned on the light. As her electric kettle boiled water for tea, she contemplated what she should spend the next few hours doing. She had gotten the most emotional task out of the way the previous night by writing notes to her friends and family. Maybe tonight she should look for fun things to do with Will that didn't cost too much and weren't too far away.

Taking her cup of hot tea, Evelyn walked into her living room and sat down on the couch. Her eyes came to rest on her journal, which she'd placed on the lower level of her coffee table with some magazines and books. She hadn't written in it for a few days, which was very out of character for her, but then again, she hadn't slept in a few days, either, so there were no dreams to write about. She picked it up, but the moment her hand met the journal, the room started spinning the same way it had at the mansion last night. Her mug crashed onto the coffee table, and Evelyn's world went black.

Coming out of the spell, Evelyn panicked. She didn't recognize the man hovering over her. Her surroundings were unfamiliar. It took her a few moments to figure out who Will was and that she was in her apartment. The blackouts were getting worse.

Evelyn sat up on the couch, shaking.

"No, no, don't move yet," Will said, laying her back down.

Groggy, Evelyn rubbed her eyes. "What time is it?" She was still confused from passing out.

"It's one fifteen."

Evelyn gazed around the room until her eyes landed on the shattered mug, pieces strewn across the table and tea dripping off the edges onto the carpet. "Oh no!" She shot up to get cleaning supplies, but Will gently pushed her back down to the couch.

"I got it," he said, heading to the kitchen.

As he cleaned up the mess, Evelyn noticed her dream journal still on the lower level of the table. She almost reached for it to keep it from getting wet but hesitated when she remembered it had been the last thing she touched before the blackout happened. She leaned back on the couch, staring at the journal. She'd had two spells in twenty-four hours, and she knew without a doubt now that she was on borrowed time. She resolved to steer clear of anything that could possibly draw a parallel to her 1919 life, since those seemed to trigger the blackouts.

Will stayed up with her the rest of the night, making sure she was all right and humoring her wish to stay awake. She lied and pretended it was because of the blackout, blaming adrenaline. In reality, she just wanted to be with him. She was so exhausted she was sure her eyes must be bulging, but after the second blackout, she was more determined than ever to stay awake. They watched a Cheaters marathon and ate popcorn until the sunrise cast an orange glow over the room.

"Wanna go to bed?" Will asked.

Evelyn didn't, but she knew he was probably tired, so she agreed. She had no plans to sleep.

Chapter 32
1919

Thomas burst through the doors to Evelyn's office building, determined to fix things between them. He hadn't heard from her since their argument at the coffee shop, and he wanted to apologize for how he'd acted the other morning. He'd been jealous and irrational, but Evelyn was in an even more impossible situation than he was. Embarrassed, Thomas hoped to clear the air and get back to normal. He wanted to be there for her during this difficult time, not add more stress to her life.

He took the stairs two at a time up to Evelyn's floor. Inhaling deeply to steady his breath, he ran through what he'd say to her. He hoped she'd even want to speak to him.

Opening the door to his uncle's office suite, Thomas peeked over at Evelyn's desk, ready for whatever angry glare or eye roll she had in store for him. He stepped further inside, confused. The desk was empty and clearly untouched. Evelyn never missed work, and Thomas knew in the pit of his stomach that something was wrong.

"Evelyn? Is that you?"

Thomas startled at his uncle's voice coming from the hallway. "Just me, Uncle Gerald!" he shouted back, closing the office door.

"I haven't seen her in two days!" the older Mr. Allen said, emerging from his office. "I can't imagine what's keeping her away. It's not like Evelyn at all!"

"No, it's not. She hasn't even called in sick?"

"No," said his uncle. "I was rather hoping you'd spoken with her."

"Unfortunately, no." Thomas walked slowly to the window. He stared at the street below. "I haven't heard from her in a couple of days. I'm afraid I may have upset her the last time we spoke."

"Ah, young love." Mr. Allen scoffed. "I'm sure she'll forgive whatever you've done. Still, I hardly think a lover's spat is a suitable reason to miss work."

"No. Something else must be wrong," Thomas said, concerned. "I have a bad feeling."

"What do you think has happened?" Mr. Allen asked, realizing for the first time something might seriously be amiss. "Surely Evelyn isn't so upset over a little argument that she's done something drastic?"

"No, no," Thomas said, quickly quelling any such thoughts. "I think she might be sick. Or maybe . . ." Thomas didn't know how to verbalize the possibilities. "I need to find her."

"How can I help?" Mr. Allen asked. "Shall we try her at home?"

"Let's go," Thomas said, already halfway out the door.

Mr. Allen hurried after him, grabbing his hat and coat, and the two men rushed to find Evelyn.

Half an hour later, they arrived at Evelyn's building. Thomas had become friendly with Edward who, upon hearing something might have happened to Evelyn, quickly accompanied Thomas and Mr. Allen up to her floor. After knocking and calling out to her with no answer, Edward fished in his pocket for the master keyring. After fumbling to find the right key, he unlocked the door, and the three men hesitantly entered Evelyn's apartment.

"Evelyn?" Thomas called out, walking slowly to the living room and scanning for any sign of her. Hearing nothing, he moved quickly toward her bedroom. He threw open the door and saw her lying motionless on the bed, fully dressed in the same outfit she'd worn the day they'd fought in the coffee shop. "Evelyn!"

He rushed to her bedside and propped himself over her, grabbing her face to check for air. "She's breathing!"

Mr. Allen joined him at Evelyn's side, picking up her right hand in his and checking for a pulse.

Thomas tried to wake her. "Evelyn, wake up!" he cried, the desperation in his voice permeating the room. "Evelyn!"

She was unresponsive, and Thomas started panicking.

"Let's get her to a hospital," Mr. Allen said, placing his hand on Evelyn's forehead to check her temperature.

Thomas wiped his hands over his face in angst. "No. No, I know who to call."

"Thomas, we don't have time! The girl needs a hospital!"

Thomas was already heading out the door. "Wait here! Watch her!" he shouted at his uncle. "I'll be right back!" The door slammed, leaving Mr. Allen to watch over Evelyn.

A while later, the apartment door burst open, and Thomas hurried inside, followed by Dr. Holstead. They rushed into Evelyn's bedroom, where Mr. Allen was sitting on the stool at the vanity. He hadn't taken his eyes off her for one minute while Thomas was gone.

Holstead checked Evelyn's pulse, just as Mr. Allen had. He lifted her eyelids. Her irises were rolled back in her head so only the whites of her eyes were showing. He turned to Thomas. "She's asleep," he said.

"Asleep?" Thomas asked, incredulous. "Why can't I wake her up?"

"Look." Holstead beckoned Thomas closer. He raised one of Evelyn's eyelids again. Thomas bent over her face. "See how the eye darts and moves around?"

Thomas nodded.

"She's dreaming. She's dreaming *deeply*."

"I don't understand," Thomas said, standing up straight.

"Dreamers can't be in two places at once, right?" Holstead asked, standing and turning to Thomas. "Well, that is to say, they can't be *conscious* in two places at once."

Thomas nodded again.

"Well," said Holstead, "in order to travel they must be asleep in one life and awake in the other."

"I'm sorry, dreamers?" Mr. Allen chimed in from the vanity stool.

Holstead glanced at Thomas. "Ah. You haven't filled him in, have you?"

"It's a long story, Uncle," Thomas said. "I'll explain later. Doctor, if she's only asleep, why does she seem like she's in a coma?"

"We had a dreamer back when we did the studies," Holstead began. "He was a bright young man, but he had a bit of a hankering for booze, if you get my drift."

Thomas wrung his hands, waiting for the explanation for what was wrong with Evelyn.

"This dreamer, Alistair, he traveled back and forth between the 1880s and his other life in the 1990s, where he became a part of a very intense crowd who attended days-long music concerts and stayed awake for hours upon hours, taking various drugs and imbibing to experience the whole event." Holstead paused and glanced at Mr. Allen, whose eyebrows were raised in confusion and disbelief.

"Anyway, Alistair would go on what he called 'benders' where he would spend days awake in the other timeline—on purpose—and would go into such a deep sleep in this life that his family thought he had a sleep disorder and sent him away to a facility where they could study his sleep and try to fix him," Holstead finished.

Nodding in understanding, Thomas sat on the bed next to Evelyn and took her hand in his. "So you're saying she's purposely staying awake in 2003 right now, and that's making it impossible for her to be awake here with us?"

"Precisely. But no one can stay awake forever, can they? She will ultimately have to wake up here."

Thomas stayed silent a while, deep in thought. "She's dying there," he eventually said. "She wants to spend time with him before she goes."

Mr. Allen jumped up from the stool, frustrated at being the only one in the room who had no idea what was going on. "Could someone please enlighten me?"

"Why don't I take you into the living room and explain, and we'll leave Thomas to sit with Evelyn?" Holstead led the way out of the bedroom.

"That would be much appreciated." Mr. Allen shut the door softly behind him.

As the older men chatted in the living room, Thomas sat beside Evelyn, staring at the barely perceptible rise and fall of her chest as she breathed. He wondered what she was dreaming about. He couldn't help but be a little jealous that she was probably with Will at this very moment, but he reminded himself that he'd started the day meaning to apologize for that very jealousy and resolved to set it aside and deal with it later.

He reached over to push a stray wisp of hair out of her face, and a lump formed in his throat. He wanted her to wake up so badly, but at the same time, she needed closure in her other life. As much as it hurt him, he knew she would never be at peace here with him if she didn't get to say goodbye to Will. He tried to placate himself with the knowledge that once she died in 2003, she'd be here with him forever, and Will would be the one missing her.

Thomas actually pitied Will, which confused him even more. Will was losing a truly amazing woman, and Thomas hoped he'd be all right after Evelyn was gone. He felt a strange kinship with Evelyn's other boyfriend. He hoped Will was making Evelyn's last days in her other life magical and that Thomas would measure up when he was all she had left. Wishing he'd left her on a better note at the coffee shop, Thomas pulled the vanity stool up to her bedside, took her hand in his, and waited for any sign of life from the woman he loved.

Chapter 33
2003

Evelyn sat on the floor of her living room in the early morning hours, staring at another photo album. She'd leafed through an entire box of albums since Will had fallen asleep. She pulled out her favorites and put them with the notes she'd written to her friends and family.

She smiled as she turned the page. There were photos of her with her parents at Disney World when she was twelve. They were all clad in bright yellow plastic raincoats, their hair soaked and the sky behind them dark with rain clouds. It had poured that day, and they'd waded through water up to their ankles as they searched for shelter in the amusement park. They'd all laughed so hard at each other in those ridiculous, overpriced ponchos. It was one of her favorite memories.

Evelyn jumped as the bedroom door clicked open. Will emerged from the bedroom, perplexed. "What are you doing?" he asked groggily.

"Nothing. Just looking at some pictures."

"Couldn't sleep?" He sat on the couch behind her and looked over her shoulder at the photo album opened on her knees.

"Not really," she lied. She'd been awake for almost forty-eight hours, and if she allowed her eyes to close, she would pass out in seconds.

"Disney?" he asked, recognizing the place in the photos. "Wow, cool ponchos!"

Evelyn reached up behind her and playfully batted at him. "Shut up!" She laughed. A huge yawn overtook her body that she couldn't hide from Will.

"You're so tired. Just come to bed," he urged. "Trust me, tomorrow we'll spend all day looking at these fantastic photos of you when you were an awkward teenager."

"You're right. I can't do this anymore."

"Do what?" he asked. "Look at photos?"

"No. Stay awake. I've been up for more than two days, Will. I'm afraid to sleep. I don't want to miss anything here."

Will slid off the couch to join her on the floor, taking the album from her and placing it on the table. He pulled her close as he spoke. "You need to sleep. I'll be here the whole time. I promise."

Out of nowhere, a sob escaped her throat. It surprised her, but she was also grateful for the release. She'd been carrying so much emotion around with her the last few days, and it was cathartic to finally express some of it. He hugged her tight.

"I'll sleep, too. At the same time. We'll set an alarm so we sleep together and wake up together, okay? We won't miss anything."

She cried harder, nodding in agreement.

"Come on, let's go." Will stood and helped her up. He led her to the bedroom, and she climbed into bed. He hurried to the other side of the bed to get in, grabbed his phone, and set an alarm for five hours later. "Let's sleep for a few hours," he said, "and when you wake up, we can do whatever you want, all right?"

Silently, she slid toward him and snuggled up to him, nuzzling her face into his chest. Soon the tears stopped, and she started drifting off. Part of her wanted to fight it, unsure that Will would fall asleep as well, but her body and mind were already too far into the process to cooperate. With Will's steady heartbeat in her ear, Evelyn finally allowed herself to succumb to the overwhelming fatigue and drifted back to 1919 for the first time in days.

Chapter 34
1919

Evelyn awoke with a loud gasp, startling even more when she found Thomas asleep on her vanity stool, his head resting on the bed. It took Evelyn a few seconds to remember that they'd parted on less than amicable terms. She wondered how he'd gotten into her apartment and what had triggered his visit. She tapped him on the shoulder.

"Thomas? Thomas, wake up."

He inhaled sharply and snapped his head up, confused momentarily about where he was. When he realized Evelyn was finally conscious, he jumped up from the stool and onto the bed to embrace her. "You're awake!"

"I'm awake," she repeated, her words muffled in his shirt as he hugged her tight. "What are you doing here?"

"I didn't hear from you after our fight, and I got worried. I had to make sure you were okay."

Just then, the bedroom door opened, and Mr. Allen and Dr. Holstead peeked in, relieved smiles plastering both their faces when they found Evelyn awake and aware.

"Ah! You've come back to us!" Holstead exclaimed happily. "You gave us all quite a scare, young lady. Especially Thomas!"

Evelyn blushed as she locked eyes with Thomas. "You were really that worried about me?" she asked.

"I couldn't think about anything else!" He badly wanted to tell her how much he loved her but didn't want to do it in front of his uncle and Holstead. Thomas said nothing and simply hugged Evelyn again.

"Ms. Moore, what happened exactly, if you don't mind my asking?" The doctor's voice interrupted Thomas and Evelyn's embrace. "You must have been awake for days in your other life to be so completely out cold here."

Evelyn was unsure how to answer without upsetting Thomas, and she was confused why they were all speaking so freely about the dreams in front of her boss. When she hesitated, Thomas interjected, "She wanted to spend as much time as possible with the people she's going to lose." Her eyes told him he was right.

"I—I just—" Evelyn took a deep breath, searching for the right words. "I thought if I stayed awake there, I could finish some things I needed to do before I—" She didn't want to say it aloud. "Before I'm gone." She knew how much anguish she was causing Thomas. "I'm sorry."

Before Thomas could answer, Holstead spoke. "Ms. Moore, staying awake for extended periods of time in any life is terrible for the body and the brain! I worry that if you continue to force yourself to avoid sleep in one timeline, you may find detriments to your wellbeing following you to the other."

Evelyn processed Holstead's warning. She hadn't considered that. "I understand, Doctor," she said. "I just wanted more time." She lowered her eyes, her sadness filling the room. "I wish there were a way."

"The only possible way to do that would be for you to sleep as much as you can here, in a healthy way, on a good schedule. But you have a job, an apartment. I'm not sure how it would work."

The room was silent for a few moments as everyone struggled over how to comfort Evelyn. Finally, Mr. Allen spoke up.

"I'm glad to give you the time you need away from the office to take care of yourself. To sleep, if that's what you need."

Evelyn smiled at him. She'd always known he was one of a kind, and she was so grateful he was being understanding, even in this rather unbelievable scenario. "I suppose the cat's out of the bag?"

"We got Uncle Gerald caught up while you were out," Thomas answered.

Evelyn turned to her boss. "I don't want to leave you without help while I do this."

"Nonsense," Mr. Allen said, waving his hand as if to shoo away the idea. "I'll call the secretarial school and they can send someone over for a day or two. It's all taken care of. Now, Doctor, how do we help Evelyn for the next few days?"

Holstead sighed, not thrilled about this path forward but understanding Evelyn's need to get closure in her other life before she was relegated permanently to this one. He couldn't imagine what she was going through, and though it went against his better medical judgment, he had to help her. "I'll have to go to my office and gather a few things. When I return, I'll explain the plan." He shuffled toward the door.

"Let me help you with a car," said Mr. Allen. "I need to get back to the office, anyway." He wished Thomas and Evelyn luck, and the two older men left the apartment, leaving the couple alone.

"I'm sorry I scared you," she said, clasping her hands in her lap.

"I thought I'd lost you."

"You haven't lost me." She reached over to run her fingers through his hair. "I'm here. And as it turns out, I'm not going anywhere."

"I know. It just feels strange that you're going through so much in the other life and I can't be there to help. I know you have Will, and I'm trying not to be jealous, but it's so hard!"

"I'm sorry." She covered her eyes with her hands. "This whole situation is so impossible!"

Thomas hugged her tightly. "I understand," he said softly. "This might be difficult, but I'm here no matter what, okay? You just get through this. I'll help as much as I can. You'll just have to let me be jealous and work that part out on my own."

Evelyn chuckled lightly, pulling away to see his face. "I really do love you, Thomas," she said. "You know that, don't you?"

Thomas paused, unprepared for such a bold proclamation from her. It was everything he'd wanted to hear since he'd initially laid eyes on her. "I love you, too, Evelyn Moore," he replied. "And I promise I'll help you with anything you need so you can have peace when you're stuck here with me for the rest of our days, okay?"

She smiled, but sadness quickly took over. "I don't want to do this. I don't know how to say goodbye to them all. No one even knows. Only Will."

"You haven't told your family?" he asked. "Your friends?"

Tears formed in her eyes as she recalled the letters she'd written in her dreams. "No. I don't want them to treat me differently or spend these last days worrying. I just want everything to be normal. I wrote them all letters. For after."

"Oh, God. Evelyn, I'm so sorry. I don't know what to say. I wish I could make it better."

"You are." She smiled weakly through the tears rolling down her face. "Just be here. Let me go through this. I'll be yours when it's all over."

"I'll be waiting," he promised, pulling her close again.

Evelyn cried into his shoulder. There were so many emotions drowning them that it seemed impossible they'd ever be able to swim up and breathe through them all, but the hardest part would be over in a few days. A fact that was simultaneously relieving, torturous, and heartbreaking.

"I'm coming back to you," she whispered. "I promise."

He nodded. The two sat in silence for a while, holding hands as more tears rolled down her already-soaked cheeks. Their love challenged the heaviness in the room, and Evelyn took comfort in the knowledge that as long as she had Thomas, she would get through the tragic days ahead.

Chapter 35
1919

When Holstead returned, he spread a collection of capsules and notes from his bag on the coffee table. He thoughtfully arranged the pills into separate doses, labeled with the day and time Evelyn should take them.

"I recommend someone stay here, in the apartment, with Ms. Moore for the duration of this . . . plan," Holstead said, looking at Thomas as if to suggest he was the obvious choice. "To ensure her safety."

Thomas sighed, staring at the heaps of medicine on the coffee table. He couldn't bear the thought of literally watching Evelyn dream about the other man she loved for days on end. He also couldn't bear to leave her alone while she did. "I'll stay, of course."

"I'll check in as often as I can," Holstead said, zipping up his bag. "I'm only a few blocks away if anything should happen."

Just then, Evelyn arrived from the bathroom in her robe, a towel around her wet hair. "Oh, you're back already!" A few days ago, she would have never dreamed of letting anyone see her in a robe, but at this point, her whole situation defied all normalcy and she no longer cared about such silly things. Holstead appeared entirely unbothered by it, in any case.

"We have a plan, Evelyn," Thomas said, moving aside to reveal the pills on the coffee table. "Dr. Holstead laid it all out here. Enough for a few days."

Evelyn examined the small groups of pills and the accompanying instructions. She was suddenly nervous. "Is this safe? This is a lot of medication."

"As safe as forced slumber can be," Holstead assured her. "If you follow my instructions to the letter, you should be just fine. *No* deviation."

Thomas and Evelyn exchanged concerned glances.

"Thomas has agreed to stay with you for your safety," Holstead said to Evelyn, hoping to ease her mind.

Evelyn waited for Thomas to confirm what Holstead said. Thomas nodded at her. "I'll stay. If it's all right with you."

"Yes, please. But only if it's not too hard on you."

"I can handle it," Thomas answered quietly.

She reached for his hand and squeezed it in hers. The warmth of his palm soothed her, and she knew without a doubt how much she would need him during the heartache ahead.

Holstead cleared his throat. "It's time I take my leave." He picked up his bag. "Please don't hesitate to call if you need me. I mean it."

"Thank you, Doctor," Evelyn said, letting go of Thomas's hand and surprising Holstead with an embrace.

Taken aback, Holstead wrapped his arms around her, patting her back as he did. He had come to care deeply about this young woman and her plight in the short time he'd known her. "It'll be all right, Ms. Moore." He pulled away. "You're going to be fine, you know. In the end."

Evelyn forced a smile. She knew she wouldn't be fine. She was losing everything in 2003. She was losing Will. She bit her lip so she wouldn't cry and thanked Holstead again.

"No thanks necessary," he replied softly. "I am sorry for all you are about to endure. Please, stay strong."

It was the first time anyone had expressed condolences to her for her own death. Evelyn wasn't sure how to process the whirlwind of thoughts and emotions that hit her as the gravity of the situation truly set in. Unable to respond verbally, she simply nodded at the doctor, hoping he understood.

Thomas escorted Holstead to the front door, leaving Evelyn in the living room studying the notes the doctor had left for her. Finally, the door clicked shut, and it was just Evelyn and Thomas alone, ready to face her devastating fate. Together and apart, simultaneously. There were no words for the situation they found themselves in, so they simply stood, wrapped in each other's arms, saying nothing. Minutes passed before either of them pulled away. Ending their embrace meant starting the heart-wrenching process ahead of them.

Finally, Thomas spoke. "How do we start?"

Evelyn thought about it briefly before she answered, "Food."

"Food?"

"I've been asleep for two days. I'm starving!" She walked toward the bedroom, and he followed her, trying to understand the plan.

"Are we cooking?"

"Oh, you're taking me out for dinner." She smiled cheekily.

"Fair enough." He chuckled. He couldn't help but fall more in love with her as she navigated this impossible situation with humor and grace. He hoped their relationship would withstand whatever happened after her dreams ended. He silently vowed to himself to do everything in his power to facilitate as seamless a transition as the circumstances would allow for Evelyn. It would be hard for them both, but for her most of all, and he had to set himself aside and prioritize her as she suffered the unimaginable loss of an entire world.

He left the room so she could dress. Out of her sight, Thomas held back tears as he mentally prepared himself for the rollercoaster he would endure alongside Evelyn over the next days, weeks, and maybe even years.

They soon took the elevator down to the lobby to head out for one last dinner date before Evelyn faced the most intense experience of her life. She'd asked Thomas not to bring up everything that was going on while they were out, and in spite of having a million things he wanted to say, he complied. They admired the city lights, marveling at what it must have been like to witness the first electric lights in the city come on in the 1880s and laughed with each other even as they made a concerted effort to ignore the elephant in the room and simply enjoy each other.

Back at home, Evelyn changed into her most comfortable nightgown, brushed her hair, and removed her makeup. She stared at her reflection in the mirror, coming to terms with the severity of the next few hours and days. She would be here, in this world, for the rest of her life after this part was over, but she'd still miss Thomas while she spent her last days with Will. She had to think of Will first, though. He was the one who would lose her for good. While Thomas waited patiently in the next room, Evelyn pulled out her journal to write one last entry before her big sleep.

I'm about to face the end of one of my lives. The end of me and Will. I have no idea how this is going to go, but I can't find words to explain how desperate I am for more experiences with him. We've been cheated out of our time together. In only a few months, he changed me so much. Our last few days together have been perfect, and I would be content to spend the rest of my life having days like them. Venturing around the city, trying new restaurants, and having conversations that provoke my mind and ignite my soul.

I almost wish I'd never gotten involved with Will so I could have spared him this heartache. Instead I've allowed him to fall in love with me, and me him, and now it's too late to release him from the hurt he is about to endure. I only hope it was as worth it for him as it was for me. In spite of causing him so much pain, he will always be the love of my lives.

Evelyn heard Thomas puttering around and closed the journal. She went into the kitchen to get a glass of water for her first sleeping pills. Thomas was standing at the living room window staring at the city street, deep in thought. She softly walked up behind him and wrapped her arms around his waist, nuzzling her face into his back. "I'm going to be okay," she promised. "*We're* going to be okay."

He turned as she loosened her grip on his waist. "I know. I just hope you won't resent me when he's gone and I'm the one you have left. I want to be enough for you. I hope I can be."

"Thomas, I don't want you to be anything more or less than you are *right now*. I couldn't ask for a better person to be by my side through this."

She locked her gaze on him. "I am so lucky to have you. When this is all over, we're going to be so happy. We just need to get through it."

He pulled her close. "I wish you didn't have to go through anything," he said. "I would rather share you with someone eighty-four years in the future for the rest of my life than have you endure such pain."

After holding each other for a while, Evelyn finally spoke. "I suppose it's time." She picked up one of the small piles of pills Holstead had left for her next to the note titled "Dose 1: First evening." Evelyn raised her glass in a mock toast and downed the handful of white tablets. Unsure what to expect, she suggested they sit in bed until she passed out.

Climbing into her bed together for the very first time, Thomas fully clothed, they held each other in silence as they waited for the pills to send her off to her dreams. Holstead's note said the first dose would last about twelve hours.

"Thank you. For being with me." Evelyn's eyelids were beginning to droop. "Don't leave."

"I'll be right here the whole time, I swear," Thomas said, trying to keep his emotions in check in front of her. He held her close. "I'll be here when you wake up."

Evelyn was too tired to answer. Giving his hand a final squeeze, the room faded to black as she drifted off to 2003 for what she knew would be some of the hardest days of either of her lives.

Chapter 36

2003

Evelyn's eyes fluttered open just before Will's alarm went off. Watching him sleep next to her, a million emotions hit her at once. Love, longing, respect, admiration. Despair. Fear of losing him.

Moments later, Will stirred as his phone chimed. He rolled over to face her while he turned it off, opening his eyes. His mouth curled into a contented smile, his hair messy from sleep and falling into his face.

"Hey, you." She pushed the stray hair away.

Sitting up, Will stretched and reached one arm around her. "You okay?" he asked, surprised she'd woken up before him. "No more blackouts, right?"

"No, no more blackouts."

"Good." He kissed her forehead. "Hey, if you're up to it, I thought maybe this afternoon I could take you to that fashion exhibit at the MET you told me about?"

Evelyn's eyes lit up. "Really?" She couldn't believe he'd remembered. She'd mentioned it in passing one night when they'd walked past the museum, but she never expected they'd actually go.

"Or we can stay home if you're not feeling good. It's up to you. You tell me what you want to do, and we'll do it, okay?"

"No!" she cried, jumping out of bed and sitting down at her vanity. "We're going!" She pulled her hair into a messy bun on top of her head. "Can we go for a walk after the museum? In Central Park?"

"Central Park it is," he said, coming up behind her and giving her a kiss on the cheek as she watched him in the mirror. "I'm ready when you are." He left Evelyn to finish getting dressed.

Later, having spent hours inside the MET and sharing lunch, the two approached Columbus Circle arm in arm, warm beverages in their free hands. They entered Central Park, which was aglow with vibrant fall colors as the leaves performed their own swan song in preparation for the winter Evelyn knew she might not live to see.

"It's beautiful, isn't it?" she said, admiring the warmly colored trees surrounding them. "This is exactly how I want to remember Central Park."

"Being here with you is exactly how I want to remember it."

"Do you want to sit?"

They sat on an empty bench, the fallen leaves gathered below crunching under their feet. Evelyn was glad for the rest. Even though she'd finally slept, she was still tired and weak. It occurred to her that it was because her body was shifting away from this timeline and toward the other one. Slowly leaving Will, little by little. The wick on her candle was burning out.

"Let's play the park game!" she suggested, hoping to distract herself. Soon they were both laughing, forgetting for a few minutes all the heartache they were about to endure.

When they arrived back at her apartment, Evelyn noted the physical toll the day had taken on her body. She'd been walking this city for years and had never been this tired. Her transition was speeding up, and it scared her.

"Can we watch something?" She sat on the couch.

"Whatever you want," he said, plopping down next to her. "You name it."

"Something funny. You choose."

As he fumbled with her DVDs, Evelyn felt the familiar signs of herself slipping away from consciousness. "Will, I don't feel right." She clutched the arm of the couch. "I think a blackout is coming."

He threw the remote down and grabbed her, carefully helping her lie down. He'd seen the blackouts a few times now, but they never got less frightening.

Once she'd come out of the spell, Will helped her sit up and kissed the top of her head. "You're fine," he assured her, knowing she wasn't.

"I'm okay," she confirmed, also lying.

The next few days were a whirlwind of beautiful moments with Will, rudely interrupted by her blackouts, which were increasing in frequency. She'd set aside a few hours to sleep, adhering to Dr. Holstead's guidelines, and taken more pills in 1919 after being awake for a little while to eat, bathe, and get some sunlight—more of Holstead's rules. She was happy to see Thomas briefly, even if it was hard to go between her two loves one right after another. She wished she could keep them both. After she'd fallen asleep and slipped away from Thomas again, Evelyn shifted her focus back onto Will.

She'd made a point to call and speak with her parents a few times over the last week, as she always did, but she kept the conversation light. She hadn't spoken to them about the dreams since they dismissed her as a child. But it was next to impossible not to break down in tears and tell them everything happening now. She hoped they wouldn't harbor too much guilt when they found out the dreams were what ultimately took her life. She addressed that in the letter she wrote for them, urging them to open their minds to new possibilities in the future. Each time she hung up the phone, she was sure to tell them how much she loved them. It wasn't something they often said aloud in her family, but it was important they hear it from her own mouth while they still could.

She and Will had agreed not to tell anyone about her dreams or the blackouts. Evelyn couldn't handle their reactions. If she allowed herself to break, she may not be able to put the pieces back together in time to spend her last moments the way she wanted to. Quietly. Peacefully. In love. With Will.

The next day, Evelyn and Will toured some of her favorite spots in the neighborhood. As they strolled the streets, she became overwhelmingly tired and asked Will if they could go home.

From the cab window on the way to her building, she drank in the city sights as they whirred by. She tried to plaster them into her memory so she could take them with her when she left this world. It broke her heart that she was too weak to walk her beloved city blocks anymore.

"Maybe we should stay home," she suggested, sadness clouding her words. "I don't want to have a blackout while we're out in public."

"You know I don't care what people think, if that's what you're worried about."

"No, I know. I care, though. If it's the last one, I want it to be just you and me."

Will couldn't help the sob that escaped his throat. She'd never said out loud exactly how she wanted to die, and it was like a knife in his heart. "I'm sorry." He tried to muffle his tears. "I'm not supposed to do this."

"Don't ever be sorry," she said, wrapping her arms around him. "There are no rules for this situation we're in."

For the first time, Will cried in front of her, releasing the depth of emotions he'd been trying to suppress for her sake for weeks. He wanted to save his tears until after she was gone, to be strong for her. Yet here she was, comforting him in the back of a yellow cab. "This is so wrong," he said, straightening up.

"What is?" Evelyn asked, tenderly stroking his neck.

"All of it! It's so unfair!"

"I know." She was lost for words. He was right. It was wholly unfair. They hadn't asked for any of it. Still, she would be forever grateful that she'd had him alongside her through this ordeal. She needed him to promise her he wouldn't let this ruin his life, but now was not the right moment.

They finally reached her building and made their way up to her apartment. They both changed into pajamas and snuggled up together under a blanket on her living room couch. Her head was pounding from the last blackout, and she wasn't sure how long she had until the next one. Or how many she even had left.

"Will," she said, lightly running her fingers across his chest. "I need to talk to you about something important."

He sat up straight, worried about what she would say.

She continued. "I want you to be okay after this is over. I want you to date again."

Will scoffed. "Yeah, right!"

"I'm serious. I get that it might take a while, but I need to know that you're going to live your life after I'm gone. You have so much to give to this world. It would mean everything to me knowing you won't give up. I don't want to be the reason you're not happy."

"*You're* the reason I'm happy, though." After a long, thoughtful pause, he continued. "Look, I'm sure I'll find happiness again somewhere, someday. But I can't promise it'll be soon, and I *know* it will never be like what we have." He didn't know what else to say, so he said what he'd always wanted to. "I'm so in love with you, Evelyn. I have been since the first day of junior year when I laid eyes on you in that lecture hall. I never thought I would be lucky enough to have you, but you've had my heart for a long, long time, and that isn't going to change no matter what timeline you're in."

"I'm in love with you, too, Will," she answered quietly, her voice cracking with emotion. "So deeply in love. I just wish it hadn't taken me so long to give us a chance."

"It doesn't matter." He pulled her close. "We're together now. These past few months have been the best of my life."

She nuzzled into him. "I want to remember us dancing in the garden with all the lights and the fountain and the music the other night." She smiled. "It was the most magical, perfect night of my entire life, and I will never, ever forget it, no matter where I am in time."

"I'm glad I could give you that memory," he whispered, burying his face in her hair. "I wish we could make more."

"Me, too." They sat in silence for a while, the moment speaking for itself. They both knew their time was running out, and the weight of their imminent doom as lovers was heavy in their air as they immersed themselves in each other's presence, committing every detail to memory. She studied his hands, strong and able but soft and tender to the touch with a little freckle on the back of the left one. She'd always remember it because she had a freckle in the exact same spot.

He breathed in the scent of her shampoo, vowing never to forget how she smelled or how she fit so perfectly into him. Her short frame was the perfect size to ball up next to him under the blanket. They soaked each other in, storing away all the tactile memories they could take with them into their unbearable fate.

Chapter 37
2003

That night and the next morning, Evelyn had two blackouts only hours apart. She and Will both knew they had very little time left together. She was getting weaker from the trauma of each episode and sensed herself actively fading from this world. Away from Will, toward Thomas. They were both wonderful men, but the pain of leaving Will forever was sure to be too much to bear. Of all the things she was about to lose, Will was the one she was most scared to live without.

They stayed at Evelyn's for the day, worried that she might have another episode. In spite of not being able to leave the apartment, she wanted to repay him for the night he'd planned for her at the mansion, so that evening she sent him to pick up takeout from her favorite Chinese restaurant while she set up a mini date for him.

When he returned, he found the apartment lights off and the space dimly lit by candles scattered around the living room. He smiled, amused and excited to find out what Evelyn had in store. He placed the takeout bag on the kitchen counter and wandered the house. "Evelyn?"

"I'm out here!"

He couldn't tell exactly where the voice had come from. The living room curtains moving caught his attention, and he realized the sliding door to the balcony was open. He went over and pushed the curtains aside.

She had decorated the balcony with dozens of flameless candles and flowers and a blanket with piles of pillows. A metal bucket filled with ice held a few bottles of his favorite beer. She was standing at the railing with her back to him, staring at the city below. The sight of the woman he loved admiring the city she adored took his breath away. Her hair was gathered at the nape of her neck, and her long, pale pink dress billowed slightly in the wind. She looked like an angel. She turned to face him, smiling. The lights from the street below danced in her eyes as she embraced him.

"I know it's not a mansion, but I wanted to do something special for you," she said, holding both his hands in hers.

"You are absolutely breathtaking," he uttered, genuinely stunned by her as the wind played softly with a few fallen curls that framed her face.

She came closer and lifted herself up on her toes to kiss him long and hard. She nestled her face in his shoulder afterward. "I've been dreaming every night my entire life, and not even my most beautiful dream has come close to how it feels being with you."

They held each other for a long time before they sat on the blanket, and she opened a beer for each of them, handing him a bottle.

He pulled her close to him, and they sat in silence for a few minutes, her head on his shoulder as they took in the sounds of the traffic and the warmth of each other.

Eventually, Evelyn lifted her head and spoke. "I won't be able to get over you. When I'm in my other life for good, I'll always be thinking of you. Wishing for you."

He rubbed her hand softly. "I'll be wishing for you, too." He kissed the thoughts right out of her head. When they pulled away, he held her face in his hands. "You're the one, Evelyn. I'll never love anyone the way I love you."

She didn't know what to say. She reached back and pressed a button on the stereo she'd hidden behind the pillows. They held each other tightly and lay on her balcony as Led Zeppelin's "Thank You" played.

"When you miss me, think of this song," she whispered in his ear. She put her head on his chest, breathing him in.

He closed his eyes and choked back the torrent of emotions that threatened to escape him at any moment. He was petrified to face life without her, and even more so knowing she hadn't actually died but was still out there somewhere, living on in another world. With another man.

A soft, cold breeze blew over the balcony. Will went inside to retrieve the throw blanket from the couch. He spread it over them on the balcony, and they curled back up as the song played in the background.

A minute later, Evelyn sat up to say something to him but stopped short. Her face went blank. Will knew she was on the verge of a blackout.

"It's okay, I've got you," he assured her, putting his arms around her.

"Will . . ." She barely got his name out before her eyes closed and her body went limp.

He held her in his arms, trying not to cry. He desperately wanted more time with her, and each second she was out was like an eternity as he waited to see if she would come back to him.

"Evelyn!" She showed no signs of life, and he pleaded breathlessly with the universe not to take her yet. "Come on, Evelyn. Wake up! Wake up!" He brushed the hair out of her face. "Evelyn, please! I love you so much. Don't go yet. Please! I'm not ready!" His heart skipped a beat when her eyelids fluttered open.

She stared at him, dazed.

"Evelyn!" His face was soaked with tears.

"Will," she whispered, lifting her hand weakly to cup his cheek.

He let out a sob when he heard her say his name, utterly relieved he hadn't lost her yet. "I love you so much. I swear I'll never love anyone as much as I love you. I don't care where we are or when, my heart will always be yours. Do you hear me?"

Silently, she reached into a pocket in her dress to retrieve something. Her fist clenched weakly, and she brought her hand over to him.

Confused, he put out his palm, and she dropped something into it. When he opened his hand and saw what it was, it absolutely broke him. The cork from their date night.

She wrapped his fingers around it. "No matter where. Or when."

"No matter where or when. I promise." He was weeping uncontrollably.

"I love you." She was struggling to speak, the dim candlelight dancing across her face.

He leaned forward and pressed his lips against hers. He kissed her as long as he could without crying. When he pulled away, her eyes were closed again. His heart shattered as he realized he had kissed her while she'd taken her last breath.

He collapsed over her lifeless figure and wailed into her chest. She was as gorgeous as ever in her long gown and soft, perfect curls splayed on the pillow under her head. Choking on his own grief, he kissed her lips again. They were still warm, but no breath came from them.

The song reached its crescendo in the background as Will wept inconsolably, cradling Evelyn's body on a balcony in 2003 while her soul left him to go to 1919 for the very last time.

Epilogue
1921

Two years later

Evelyn turned out the lights as she entered the dining room, holding a large birthday cake laden with lit candles. "Okay, birthday boy, time to sing!"

Setting the cake in front of Thomas, Evelyn leaned down to give him a peck on the cheek. As they sang, she marveled at the group of people in the room and how much her life had changed in the last two years.

The first few weeks and months after losing her other life had, as expected, been the hardest Evelyn had ever faced. She grieved Will while trying to be respectful of Thomas, which had proven a fine line to walk. Thomas was the picture of patience and grace as he supported her through it, in spite of how complicated it was for him. She eventually pulled herself out of the depths of her sorrow and embraced her full-time life in 1919. She and Thomas advanced their relationship at a pace that made Evelyn comfortable, but their friends and family were eager to see the two engaged.

Calvin moved to Connecticut, according to the rumor mill, after losing his fortune in the city, and went to work for his uncle's law firm instead. Evelyn was glad she didn't have to worry about running into him around every corner anymore or that he would take his jealousy out on Thomas again.

With Thomas by her side, Evelyn worked through the grief and figured out how to live with the memories that would always haunt her no matter how much time passed. She still thought about Will and her family and friends in 2003 all the time. She often took walks in Central Park near Columbus Circle and sat on a bench at Washington Square Park, silently assigning fake jobs and names to those who passed by, laughing to herself and hoping Will would have laughed along with her. She felt him when she visited the places both worlds shared. She wondered if he ever went to those places in the other life, to remember her the same way she remembered him. She pictured him sitting next to her in his own timeline when she was there in hers.

It took Evelyn some time to work out her affections for both Thomas and Will after she left her dream life, but she'd gotten to a place where the thought of Will didn't make her cry anymore but rather smile at the memories they'd had the privilege of making.

Thomas was such a steady support and such a kind, loving presence in her life that she couldn't help but fall for him harder and faster as he guided her through her darkest time. She was grateful for him and found peace in being his partner. He listened to her just as Will always had. She knew Will and Thomas were kindred spirits and liked to think they'd have gotten along if they'd ever had the chance to meet.

As the birthday song wrapped up, Evelyn scanned the room one more time. She smiled at the people who had started as business associates, doctors, and acquaintances and had become her family. Dr. Holstead and Ms. Brooks, who came over for dinner at least once a week, became fast friends of hers and Thomas's. Mr. Allen, who now insisted Evelyn refer to him as simply Gerald, had practically become family. Her job hadn't changed, and they often spent holidays and weekends all together instead of their previous Monday through Friday schedule. Nancy Allen was the mother Evelyn had always wished for in the city, and the two became close. Her friends, Ada, Emily, and Lily, who had taken to Thomas immediately, were still her go-to support system when she needed advice she couldn't get anywhere else.

Evelyn had made a cozy little life for herself here in this timeline, and though she missed the people from her other world so much it hurt sometimes, she appreciated this life for what it was and for what it was becoming.

Thomas blew out his candles, cracking a joke about calling the fire department for all the flames. He turned around in his chair, motioning for

Evelyn who was behind him to come closer. "You wanna tell them?" he asked quietly.

"You do the honors." She squeezed his shoulder.

Standing, Thomas tapped his fork against his glass of champagne. Everyone fell silent, watching him expectantly.

"First, I want to thank you all for being here to celebrate my gaining a few more gray hairs this year." The room broke out in hushed laughter. "This has been a very busy year for Evelyn and me." He put his arm around her. "I became a doctor, *finally*!" The group cheered at his accomplishment. "And," Thomas said loudly, signaling he had more to say, "last night, I asked Evelyn to be my wife!"

The room erupted into excited chatter as everyone hugged Evelyn and Thomas, peppering them with questions about their impending nuptials. Ms. Brooks and Nancy tearfully embraced, thrilled to start planning a wedding. Evelyn's friends huddled around her, eagerly examining her engagement ring. Evelyn was overjoyed and touched that all these people cared so much about hers and Thomas's happiness, but she couldn't forget that just a few years ago, she'd hoped to have a moment just like this with Will. Still, she marveled at how wonderful a life she'd created for herself here with a man who loved her unconditionally, and she was determined to make the most of it.

The next day, Evelyn kissed Thomas goodbye, leaving him at his office to run some errands. Walking down the city streets, she basked in the warm sunlight of the afternoon and took a deep breath. She reveled in these precious moments alone. She loved her friends and family, and of course Thomas, but she also needed time to reflect every now and then. To remember what she'd lost when she'd left her other life.

After she'd visited the grocer and the post office, Evelyn spent an hour strolling through the neighborhood, thinking about 2003. She wondered what Will was doing in what was now 2005. She wished she knew if he'd graduated with honors or if he'd gotten a job at the United Nations like he'd always wanted. She hoped he was happy, whatever he was doing. Even if that meant he'd moved on to loving someone else.

Lost in her daydreams about what might be happening in her other world without her, Evelyn headed toward home. Suddenly, all thoughts left her head, and her heart dropped as a male figure stepped from a car in front of the apartment building ahead.

The man jogged to the passenger side, opening the door for a beautiful young woman dressed as though she'd just walked off a Hollywood red carpet. The man closed the door behind the glamorous woman and turned, finally noticing Evelyn. He tipped his hat to greet her politely then caught up with his gorgeous female companion. Evelyn was pinned to the spot and felt like she couldn't breathe. All she could do was open her mouth to whisper his name as he disappeared inside the building.

"Will?"

THE END

Acknowledgement

First, let me answer the number one most frequently asked question I've received since becoming a writer: It's pronounced Spee-vack. Rhymes with "Ski, Jack!" Moving on.

When you wake up one day at almost 40 years old and decide you want to be a writer when you grow up, one thing becomes very clear, very quickly: you can't do it alone.
I couldn't have done a single minute of work on this novel if it hadn't been for the undying and multi-faceted support of my favorite human of all time, my husband, Dan. I am good at writing, and he is good at everything else. No, seriously. From spreadsheets to marketing plans to putting ink in the printer, he helped make this novel possible. I am so lucky to have him.

This book is for my children as much as it is for me. Bryce, Ava and Austen, always follow your dreams. Even if it takes years.

I would be remiss if I didn't give a major portion of the thanks for this book to my amazing editor, Jessica Fortenberry. I believe my exact words to her were that this book would be "a half-baked dumpster fire" without her, and I stand by that statement. She has made me a better writer.

To my parents, in-laws, family and friends, who have encouraged me, cheered me on and followed my journey as I brought this novel to life: I love and appreciate every one of you. Thanks to Getcovers Design for putting up with my zillion changes on the cover art. I will be back again and again. To Katie and Chris Evers, for their overwhelming generosity and for believing in me so much. And to everyone else who has helped me along the way, you have my eternal gratitude. I hope reading this book brings you as much joy as it brought me to write it.

Dream on.

About the Author

Laura Spivak is a new author who lives in Maryland, USA, with her husband and three children. Laura has previously worked as a news writer and has had several articles featured on a popular parenting website, but has always dreamed of writing a full-length novel. Dreams do come true!

You can connect with me on: www.lauraspivak.com

Coming in 2024 by Laura Spivak...

Book 2
When Evelyn Sleeps: Daydreams